HEART OF THIRST

FELICITY CONSTANTINE

Author's Tranquility Press
Marietta, Georgia

Copyright © 2022 by Felicity Constantine.

All rights reserved. No part of this publication may be reproduced, distributed or transmitted in any form or by any means, including photocopying, recording, or other electronic or mechanical methods, without the prior written permission of the publisher, except in the case of brief quotations embodied in critical reviews and certain other noncommercial uses permitted by copyright law. For permission requests, write to the publisher, addressed "Attention: Permissions Coordinator," at the address below.

Felicity Constantine/Author's Tranquility Press
2706 Station Club Drive SW
Marietta, GA 30060
www.authorstranquilitypress.com

Publisher's Note: This is a work of fiction. Names, characters, places, and incidents are a product of the author's imagination. Locales and public names are sometimes used for atmospheric purposes. Any resemblance to actual people, living or dead, or to businesses, companies, events, institutions, or locales is completely coincidental.

Ordering Information:
Quantity sales. Special discounts are available on quantity purchases by corporations, associations, and others. For details, contact the "Special Sales Department" at the address above.

Heart Of Thirst/Felicity Constantine
Paperback: 978-1-957208-26-8
eBook: 978-1-957208-27-5

First off, congratulations on writing a humorous, original novel! Your characters were intriguing and distinctive, and the dialogue was spot on. The characters were all very well-defined. Their voices were distinctive, and you did an excellent job characterizing Danielle in particular. Well done!

I think the dramatic tone you were aiming for was generally conveyed very well. I just want to reiterate that I found the book amusing and original! Your characters were interesting, and your plot was organized and entertaining. I wish you all the best for this manuscript and future books.

— Wes, Editor

The book tells an entertaining story with engaging characters. The main characters—Danielle, Jess, Max, and Ted are all likeable and well-thought-out characters with interesting back stories. The love triangle element of the story is resolved in a terribly tragic way at the climax of this book, giving Part I a more-or-less complete story arc while laying a pretty good foundation for Part II. It's very well done.

The story reads well. The writing flows nicely and is easy to understand.

—Ray, Editor

This is a very fast paced, easy-reading story about Danielle ___ a young, black attorney and her impressions of the men she has dated or should date. Her opinions and those of her best friend, Jessica, are insightful and at times hilarious, but true. Through their eyes we see the different men they have met and how they feel about them. Surely, everyone has met some of these types. The romantic scenes she describes are easy to picture and steamy!

The author has a way with words that makes the reader understand the family values and relationships that Danielle and her colleagues and friends have encountered in their lives. As you get to know each character, sometimes you cheer for one, later rooting for another.

The twists of the story make this book a page turner that you won't want to put down. Can't wait for Volume two!

— Cary Gandolfi

Table of Contents

Book One *5*
Chapter 1 .... *6*
Chapter 2 .... *19*
Chapter 3 .... *40*
Chapter 4 .... *46*
   Love Is a Fleeting Fancy *50*
Chapter 5 .... *55*
Chapter 6 .... *75*
Chapter 7 .... *78*
Chapter 8 .... *95*
Chapter 9 .... *119*
Chapter 10 .... *134*
Chapter 11 .... *140*
Chapter 12 .... *152*
Chapter 13 .... *161*
Chapter 14 .... *163*
Chapter 15 .... *175*
Chapter 16 .... *177*

Book One

Danielle

Chapter 1

The alarm sounded at 5:30 a.m., as it did every day. Danielle rolled over and shut it off, deciding to lie there a moment before starting her morning ritual of prayer and meditation. She reflected on the life she had left behind with Carl Palmer. She was never again going to put up with any man cheating on her or monopolizing her time. She was determined to be happy and take things as they came. Dating was not on her agenda, but when it was, it would be on her terms.

Experience had taught her that there was no such man as Mr. Right. All that existed was someone you were willing to take a chance on getting to know. She seriously thought that maybe she should start dating white men. At least with a white man, she knew what to expect. White men appeared to be more open and honest with their true feelings. They seemed to speak from the heart and tell you exactly what was on their minds.

Danielle wanted to be rich, famous, and successful. Secretly, R, F, and S were the three things Danielle desired.

The three goals she set while in college. She didn't need financial security from any man, white or black.

Danielle had come into her own before the age of twenty- six. Not even twenty-seven yet, she was the youngest attorney at O'Reilly, Thorngill, Rothchild, and Ziegerman. Immediately after graduating from Nova High School at the age of seventeen, she enrolled in and completed the political science program at Nova University in three and a half years.

While in school Danielle had one goal in mind: graduate from Yale Law School before her twenty-fourth birthday. Why shouldn't she? An honor student and very focused, she knew what she wanted. She graduated from Yale at twenty-three and took a job at the state attorney's office.

The two years she spent there proved to be a godsend. That was where she met Ted O'Reilly-while prosecuting one of Ted's clients at the Broward County Courthouse, a case she won. Ted was impressed with her skills, and he wanted her on his team. Everything she had ever dreamed of fell into place.

She looked around the room to admire and thank God for all she had and the wonderful life he had given to her. God had truly blessed her. She owned a beautiful five-bedroom, English- style home on the intercostals in Fort Lauderdale. The entire home was decorated in white. Even her bedroom was tailored for a princess: pure white furniture, lacy bed coverings with matching curtains, and gold fixtures throughout the house that added a perfect touch. Her contract with Baily's on Sunrise Boulevard had ended, and she'd decided not to renew it. She was happy not to have to make the trip across town every Saturday. She could now work out in the gym located upstairs in the west wing of her spacious home.

The phone rang. Danielle was so deep in thought that she almost didn't hear it. As she reached to pick up the receiver, the call went to her answering machine.

"Dani, wake up. Are you still asleep?"

Danielle recognized the voice of her best friend, Jessica, whom she'd known since preschool, and picked up the receiver.

"I'm awake. I was just lying here thinking."

"I hope you weren't thinking about CP."

"No, I was not. Well... he did cross my mind."

"What were you thinking about?"

"If you must know, I was thinking about white men."

"Why were you thinking about them?"

"I have decided that the next man I date will be white."

"Are you serious?"

"Very! I've had such bad luck with black men. Perhaps dating outside of my race will work for me."

"Just be happy, no matter whom you date."

"Is that your advice?"

"Yes, it is," said Jess. "Dani, you know you are beautiful inside and out. You've got looks and a body to die for. Not only that, but you are an attorney with a six-figure income, and you're highly intelligent. My friend, you are what they call prime stock. Everyone knows it's true. Carl was just too blind to see it. It's his damn loss."

"What are you doing up at this time of morning anyway?" Danielle asked.

"Look at you changing the subject."

"I'm not changing the subject."

"Yes, you are, but that's not why I called. Guess who called me late last night asking about you."

Danielle rose from her pillow and placed her feet on the floor. "Someone called you about me?" she asked, surprised.

"They sure did," replied Jess

"What did they want to know?"

"How did Danielle get a house on the intercostals? She hasn't been out of school that long. Everybody knows she didn't make that kind of money the two years she worked at the state attorney's office. What man is she dating to buy her a house like that?"

"How pitiful. They're keeping up with my life and career. That's nice to know. Well, what did you tell them?"

"Don't worry. I didn't say a word, Dani. Your secret is safe with me."

"I know you wouldn't violate a confidence, especially mine."

"I couldn't violate it if I wanted to. I don't even know the fake name you're using."

"I told you, Jess that's for your protection."

"Yeah, and why is that? I had to find out about this missing link clearly by accident."

"What do you mean? I told you about the assumed name. Not giving you the actual name was my way of protecting you."

"Were you really protecting me? Don't you mean protecting yourself?" Jess laughed.

"Whatever," Danielle replied.

"Girl, I know, and I am glad you are looking out for me. That is why I told them that they're just jealous, and that they need to get a life and stop worrying about you. Out of everyone in our neighborhood who grew up with us, you are the only one who made it big. Almost everyone else is either on crack, living with a cracked-out man, or dealing with baby mama drama."

"That's sad to hear."

"Don't go feeling sorry for them. They made their choices in life, and you made yours."

"Jessica, are you going to tell me who called you?"

"No. I'm going to let you go so you can get ready for work." "Come on and tell me. Who was it?"

"Girl, go to work. I'm not telling you anything. I'm hanging up." "Don't you hang up this phone until you tell me who called you last night," Danielle demanded.

"You really want to know?" asked Jessica.

"Yes! I do."

"Okay, it was Santa Claus."

"Santa Claus? What are you talking about? What about Santa Claus?"

"That's who called me."

"Jess, stop playing."

"I'm not playing. I'm serious," said Jess.

"Yeah, right."

"Okay, what is Santa Claus's famous saying?" Jess asked.

"Ho, ho, ho," Danielle said.

"Now, who is the biggest ho you know?"

"Sharon Cason?"

"Sharon's new name is Santa Claus, 'cause she's a ho, ho, ho.

She's such a ho that they added a new category for her blood type.

"You know your ass is crazy."

"I'm serious. Just listen to me. We got Type A, Type B and Type 0 blood. Now we got Type Ho blood. Sharon's blood type is ho positive. Sharon is a true three-D ho."

"What is a three-D ho?" Danielle asked. "She is a damn desperate dame," Jess said.

"Oh my God!" Danielle screamed with laughter as she fell back, bumping her head on the headboard.

"Jess, you are crazy. Where do you come up with this stuff? You know you missed your calling. You should have been a comedian."

"You're always telling me to take the diplomatic approach, but I should have cursed her ass out. I need to show you how to curse a bitch out and make them think that you're giving them a compliment."

"How would I do that?"

"If I had said to Sharon S-Y-B-A-D, I am not telling her she's bad. I'm saying, sit your black ass down. If I should say S-Y-A-D to anyone who is not black, I'm simply saying, sit your ass down."

"Thanks for my lesson." Danielle laughed.

"Now that you've had your laugh for the day, you'd better get ready for work. Oh, one more thing. Since you are planning on dating white men, I suggest that you start with those fine bosses of yours. I would if I were you."

"You would not."

"You should date all of them!"

"Then you'll be calling me Santa Claus."

"No, I wouldn't. I'll call you Santa's little helper."

"What do you want me to do-take Sharon's place?"

"You could never be a full-fledged Santa. Besides, having you for a girlfriend would be a plus for him."

"Why do you say that?"

"Because you wouldn't kiss and tell."

"You think you got ESP now?"

"No, I just know you. You wouldn't get diarrhea of the mouth."

"Oh, I wouldn't?" asked Danielle.

"Face it, you're no Monica Lewinski or Paula what's-her-face."

"Paula who?"

"You know-the one who accused Clinton of sexual harassment."

"Isn't she the one who got a nose job and makeover?" asked Danielle.

"The one and only!" said Jess.

"Oh yeah, her name was Paula. Hey, Jess, don't you think it's ironic how no one remembers her full name?"

"Monica was famous for a blowjob, and Paula became famous for a nose job. They were both made famous for the jobs that gave them the most media coverage." Jess continued,

"Ladies and gentlemen, in this corner we have Monica the blowjob, and in this corner, we have Paula the nose job. And the winner is...Monicaaaa!"

Danielle rolled around on her bed, laughing to the point of tears. "Girl, you are really crazy."

"Why I got to be crazy? People don't understand me. I'm just saying," said Jess. "You heard the saying 'game recognize game'? Well, a ho recognizes another ho."

"What in the world are you talking about, Jess?" asked Danielle. "I'm trying to tell you."

"Tell me what?" Danielle asked. "I got a little Santa in me."

"Girl, please, when did you start dating?"

"The question is how many," Jess said, snickering. "Please, you're not a whore."

Jess pretended to cry and asked, "Why can't I be a ho? I can be a ho if I want."

Now they were both laughing.

Danielle had tears rolling down her cheek. "Girl, you are crazy. I can't remember when I laughed so much." She looked over at the clock, which now read 6:15 a.m. "Jess, I really have to get going. I have to be in the office by nine o'clock for a meeting."

"Wait a minute. Let me tell you this before you go."

"What?"

"You know why black men love Wild Bill?" "Who is Wild Bill?"

"Bill Clinton, girl. Stay with me now."

"Okay, Jess, why do black men love Bill Clinton?" "Because Bill got game."

"What game is that?" asked Danielle.

"He's a playa."

"Bill Clinton is not a player."

"Yes, he is! Check it out. Wild Bill is a four-F man."

"God! What is a four-F man?"

"Black men have made Bill Clinton an honorary member of the four-F club. Bill loves the ladies."

"Bill loves his wife, Hillary."

"Bill got game. He finds them, fool them, fuck them, and then he forgets them," said Jess.

"Jess, you said the F word."

"I know. I feel liberated."

"Liberated from what?"

"You are talking to the sole owner of A Touch of Class Beauty Salon."

"Oh, my God! Jess, that's wonderful. I'm so happy for you."

"It was the loan I got from you that made it possible," said Jess.

"We have to celebrate. Where would you like to go? My treat," Danielle said.

"You don't have to do that," said Jess.

"I want to do this for you."

"Dani, you've already loaned me thirty thousand dollars, and you never asked if or when I could pay you back. You've done more than enough."

"Jess, what if I tell you that you never have to pay me back?" "Are you crazy? I can't let you do that, Dani. I asked for fifteen thousand dollars because I was borrowing the other half from the bank. When you doubled it, I didn't need to borrow from the bank. Besides, that's too much money for you to just give me."

"You're not just anyone, Jess. You are my best friend. Remember, I have a six-figure income. I paid cash for my house, and that new Mercedes was a gift when I signed on with the firm. I never have to touch my paychecks, so the money is just sitting in the bank. I'm living off the checks I receive under my assumed name."

"You have to let me pay you back."

"Jess, all I want from you is to tell me that you got Melanie to sign all the papers that I had drawn up before you gave her the money."

"She said she was in a hurry. She promised to come by the shop first thing this morning to sign the papers."

"You're telling me you placed thirty thousand dollars in Melanie's hands for her share of the shop without getting her to sign the documents that the transaction ever took place? Please tell me that you at least had one witness present who can verify that you bought her out."

"Slick was there."

"Who is Slick? Does he work in the shop?"

"No, he's Melanie's boyfriend."

"Where were the other people who work in the shop? Weren't they there?"

"Melanie wanted me to give her the money outside. She said she was afraid of being robbed if someone knew she had that much money on her."

"She convinced you that transacting business outside was safer?"

"We sat in the back of Slick's car and made the transaction."

"My God! Jess, it's possible you were set up. It was much safer for her to be given the money inside the shop rather than outside."

"Melanie insisted that we go outside."

"That doesn't make any sense."

"What do you mean it doesn't make any sense?"

"It doesn't add up," Danielle said.

"It doesn't?"

"No! It does not add up. This is the same Melanie whom you were desperate to end your business ties with. This is the same person who didn't turn in money receipts from the business and stole money from the register." Danielle shook her head. "Maybe things aren't clear because I can't concentrate on this right now. I really got to get to the office. I can't be late for my meeting. I'll handle Miss Melanie and Mr. Slick before the day is over. They took advantage of you, and I promise they will not get away with it. Don't do anything, Jess. Let me deal with those two crooks. Now, I have to jump in the shower and get to the office. I'll call you later."

"Okay, I'll wait on your call," said Jess.

"Bye," said Dani.

Max Thorngill

Ted, Ross, and Chad

Chapter 2

Danielle arrived at the office and walked into the conference room just as the meeting was about to start. Carmen, Ted's legal secretary, always had everything set up prior to the start of each meeting, and the seating arrangements were preselected.

Two attorneys working together on a case were seated across from each other to collaborate and present their progress report. This seating arrangement was similar to a bidding Swiss card game in which one sits across from a partner and signals whether to go low or high to win the game. No one played the game better than Danielle and Max.

Senior partner Ted O'Reilly began the meeting by announcing the opening of the London office. Danielle could not help staring at Ted, reflecting on the conversation she'd had with Jessica earlier that morning. She had to admit that she did in fact have four super-fine bosses. Ted, one of four senior partners, was tall, tanned, and handsome, and he had brown hair with a little gray around the edges. He looked as if he should be a character in a Harlequin romance novel. He was super Fine with a capital F.

Danielle looked around the room until her eyes stopped on Max Thorngill, another senior partner who was just as fine as Ted. Max was also tall, with blond hair that dropped below his ears. To say that he was good looking would be a definite understatement. The man was simply gorgeous.

Danielle was embarrassed at the thoughts that crossed her mind. As her mind continued to wander, she suddenly realized that she had not paid attention to anything Ted was saying. This was a first for her. Perhaps Danielle's inability to concentrate today was partially due to Jessica's dilemma with Melanie, or maybe it was her wondering what it would be like to be with a white man.

Chad Rothchild, another senior partner, looked at Danielle and smiled. She returned the gesture. Why is he smiling at me? she thought. Chad was without a doubt a super-fine white man with a nice, nice body. He looked like a male model with rippled abs and dark brown hair to match his good looks. He must work out. His body screamed muscles, and his suits were perfectly tailored. Danielle dared not look in his direction again for fear he may somehow guess what she was thinking. But, oh, how tormenting it was to keep her eyes off him. He was what Jess would call a panty wetter. Just looking at him was enough to get any woman excited.

Danielle took a deep breath and leaned forward. Ross Ziegerman, who was also a senior partner, was now looking at her, smiling. Danielle blushed and scribbled the words Campbell Soup on her notepad. Mr. Campbell Soup-that would be the perfect name for Ross. Danielle wondered if he tasted as good as he looked. Ross was so fine he looked like a Ken doll: blond hair, blue eyes, and a warm smile. He was quite the male specimen. Unable to stop critiquing her bosses, she hummed, "That's why Campbell soups are mmm, mmm good."

She was horrified when everyone in the conference room laughed. She thought they all heard her humming. Oh my God! How could I be so stupid? This can't be happening to me. God, please help me concentrate. I need to keep my mind on this meeting. Dear God! Please don't let Ted regret hiring me.

"What do you think, Danielle?" Ted asked.

What do I think? Obviously, they had laughed about something Ted had said and not at her humming. She was relieved.

Ted had announced that the firm had opened a London office, and that he and the other senior partners will meet to discuss choosing one of them to help set up that office. Danielle knew he absolutely hated it if an attorney didn't take the meetings seriously. Not being able to answer a question in a meeting could get someone in trouble. It was imperative that everyone remain alert and actively participate. Danielle could tell that Ted knew she hadn't been listening. He looked at Danielle and smiled. "Danielle, humor me. You use to laugh at my jokes. I said this will be a trip of a lifetime. But it surely wouldn't be a vacation."

Danielle looked at Ted, shook her head, and laughed.

"So, what do you think?" Ted asked again.

Danielle, looking around the room before she replied, "I think that the attorney chosen to go to London would have to work hard to complete the project ahead of time. This should create enough free time to turn the trip into a vacation."

The senior partners looked at each other, nodding in agreement. Danielle looked at Ted O'Reilly, the head of the firm, and tightened her lips as if to say, "Mum's the word."

She immediately opened the file she'd brought to the meeting to review her report. She knew Ted had covered for her. Making a joke was his way of giving her a heads-up to prepare. He had never had to cover for her before, but today he seemed to sense that something was wrong. She was not focused, and somehow Ted knew it. Amazingly, Danielle and Ted seemed to connect on a mental and spiritual level.

Because of where she and Max were seated today, next to Ted, she would have to go first with her progress report on how her court case was going. At these weekly meetings, the partners offered advice and made suggestions as to the best way to handle a case.

The seating arrangements were arranged accordingly. The male attorneys sat on the right side of the table, and the female attorneys sat on the left. Ted was seated at the head of the table, and to his immediate right were always the other three partners and then associate attorney Juan Alvarez. At the very end, the secretaries sat with their pads and pens. Seating could change depending on the urgency of the cases and how far into the cases the attorneys might be, and whether they needed any help or advice.

On this day, Max Thorngill was seated next to Ted O'Reilly. Chad Rothchild was next to Max; Ross Ziegerman was next to Chad; and Juan was next to Ross. To Ted's left was Danielle; next to Danielle was Caroline Redman, then Lisa Chin, and then Rosario Perez, a female attorney who recently returned to the firm.

Rosario had just graduated from law school at age thirty-five. She had been working as a paralegal with the firm for five years but always wanted to be an attorney. She and Danielle had become fast friends. As soon as one of them came in from court, one was looking for the other. They were inseparable, and you would often see the two of them whispering and laughing in Danielle's office. Everyone knew it had to be about men.

Ted, making sure Danielle had plenty of time to review her report, continued to talk about the opening of the London office. "The final decision has not been made. However, there is the possibility of selecting two of you to accompany me to London. We have not arrived at a decision. But the person who gets to go will only have two weeks to get ready. You will have to make sure you have your business in order before the trip, as you will be out of the country for two months. One more thing: Danielle, we're going to be working late tonight."

Even though Danielle was partnered with Max, Ted always seemed to find something that required Danielle's help. Ted didn't have a partner, so he was free to enlist help from any of the associate attorneys. Yet he never monopolized anyone's time but Danielle's.

Ted had never been married, but the talk around the office was that he was dating Leslie, another attorney who lived and worked in Miami. She had been trying to get him to the altar, but he was standing his ground. As the story went, she had broken up with him several times because he wouldn't commit.

Apparently, Leslie had tried every sneaky device known to woman and man. Once she even claimed she was pregnant, and they say Ted told Leslie he was excited about the baby, but he wasn't sure if it was true. Ted knew Leslie to be a manipulative compulsive liar and only God knew how this would play out. He had a meeting with the partners and explained to them what was going on, and they agreed to cover his court appearances. He had Carmen reschedule all of his appointments for the day. He wanted to rush to Leslie side and take her to the doctor to confirm the pregnancy.

The truth came out when they met at her house. They got into a terrible argument because Leslie refused to go to the doctor. She ended up telling Ted there was no need to go to the doctor because she wasn't pregnant. It would seem that Ted would be upset after going through another round of lies with Leslie. But according to office gossip, he was a bit relieved not to be tied down to someone who would do something like that to tie a man down. They stopped dating for a while until Leslie begged Ted to take her back. They had an on-again and off-again relationship until Ted decided to end it for good.

The story on gorgeous Max was that he had married his high school sweetheart right after high school; a marriage that his parents never wanted to take place. She complained about his studies to become a lawyer. The complaining got worse when he became a senior partner. Max was an only child and wanted children, but Natalie didn't want to ruin her figure. She told him to wait until she turned thirty, and then they could have a baby. She turned thirty and adamantly refused to allow Max to experience the joy of becoming a father. Max just threw himself into his work; he got with his three buddies from Harvard Law School and started the firm.

It was said that the real reason Natalie didn't want children was because she was having an affair with her married boss; a job she had found only because she said she was bored. How bored was she? She worked only two hours a day. She didn't have to work, and Max never wanted her to. Supposedly, when Max found out about the affair, he told her that a baby would have kept her busy and said, "I would have been home with you and our child because I love you." He walked out and never went back for anything until he bought her a condominium on Fort Lauderdale Beach. Max moved Natalie out, and then he moved back into the house.

Natalie was always screaming that she was afraid Max would cheat because of his good looks. She just knew that women would not leave him alone. But from what Danielle had seen of her at office parties, Natalie was drop-dead beautiful. An extremely gorgeous woman, she should have been a model- she looked like a blonde Brooke Shields. Max apparently never cheated on her. He was so in love with his wife and always told women that he was married.

Max was overheard saying that women just didn't excite him, and that they were boring and had no conversational skills. He jokingly said he saw a commercial once in which the guy asked the girl out for a date, and she refused because she had plans to wash her hair. "That's how I feel about other women. I could find something better to do with my time. I'd rather read a law book," he said. The fact was that he was so in love with Natalie that, as he stated, his wife was the only one who turned him on.

Rumor had it that Max gave Natalie one million dollars, even though he didn't have to. When she thought that another woman would steal her husband, she had him draw up a legal document stating that if one of them cheated, that person would walk away with nothing. Everyone at the firm believed that whereas Natalie didn't have anyone to keep her on the straight and narrow, Max had Jackie, his secretary, in his corner. Max would never do anything that would cause him to lose Jackie's love and respect. Not when he was a kid and she was working for his parents, and not now that he's an adult and she's working for him.

Natalie was now on Jackie's shit list, and she was not going to win. Apparently, Ted had begged Max not to sign a document of such magnitude. Yet Max didn't seem to have a problem signing because he knew he would never cheat on Natalie. He was so in love with her that he didn't mind signing it just to show her that he would be willing to lose and give up everything he had worked so hard for all these years, plus everything that his parents had left him. Wow! A good and faithful man, and now he was single. Natalie did get pregnant-no, not by Max, but by her married boss who refused to leave his wife.

Jackie, a young-looking black woman in her fifties, was Max's secretary. She was a single mom who had never been married. She reminded Danielle of Wanda Sykes. She looked like Wanda -really pretty-and talked plenty of trash. Listening to Jackie, Danielle could just picture Wanda Sykes doing one of her comedy routines. There was never a dull moment with Jackie around.

The secretaries had all gotten themselves in trouble at one point for trying to take their lunch and breaks at the same time as Jackie. They loved to hear her jokes and listen to her stories about Max when he was a kid. As long as no one was telling lies or backstabbing someone, office gossip could be very enlightening.

Jackie kept everyone laughing with all of her funny stories. They made a schedule so that they could all take turns having lunch with Jackie. After all, there was a zero-absentee rate in the office; none of the office staff no longer missed work or came in late. Actually, no one ever get sick since Jackie been there. She set up her office at the firm to be near Max, three years ago, when Max lost his mom and dad.

It was heard that they paid Jackie one hundred thousand dollars a year. Supposedly this was because she was still the office manager at his parents' real estate office as well as the manager at the law firm.

Jackie had always been the office manager for the firm, but she was never seen. Paychecks were signed by Jackie Chambers, and whenever the clerical staff got warnings for something they did or didn't do, it was from the Dragon Lady, Jackie. They talked about how they would often get dragon emails for coming to work late or calling in sick. If they screwed up by typing the wrong information on a case, missing filing dates, not returning clients' calls, or causing any inconvenience by not giving any of the lawyers their messages, they caught hell. How did Jackie become so damn efficient? She didn't miss a beat.

Max had not wanted to close his parents' real estate office, so he asked Jackie to stay there and keep an eye on things. However, she insisted that she was going to be wherever he was in order to take care of him, which she did. But Jackie acted as a mother to all the partners. Maybe that was why they trusted her with everything.

The fact that Max was such a good kid who never got into trouble was partly due to his being around Jackie. Max really was wonderful. He ate one hot meal a day, which consisted of the leftovers from whatever Jackie cooked the night before. He would often try to eat just a salad or fruit in the evening. The office used to wonder why she brought him food every day. Now everyone knew that the man loved soul food.

Jackie looked out for and protected Max as if he were one of her sons, and Max loved her, too. He was a rich white boy who came from old money. His parents and grandparents were land developers who owned a lot of real estate. Through the years, he spent a lot of time at Jackie's house with her family. Jackie wasn't just Max's parents' office manager; they treated her like family. She worked for them for thirty-five years before they died in a plane crash three years ago on their way back to the States after vacationing in Japan.

Instead of mourning and standing by her man, Natalie acted. as if it were time for her to party. The day after the funeral, Natalie took two of her girlfriends and flew to New York. As she put it, she needed to relieve some stress by shopping, and she wanted to see a Broadway show. She left Max alone for two weeks to grieve over his parents. He packed a suitcase and stayed at Jackie's, waiting for Natalie's return. That's when everyone found out just how close Max and Jackie were and how much he loved his secretary.

The truth was that Jackie had always played the role of mother to Max. Jackie had been taking care of Max since he was three years old. When Max was at Jackie's, he was in the hood, and he felt right at home. Everyone saw him as that white boy Mrs. Jackie raised. Max's parents couldn't keep him home; he wanted to live with Jackie and only visit his parents on the weekend.

His parents wanted to keep their son happy and safe, so they offered to buy Jackie a house in a better neighborhood. However, she wouldn't move. She loved her little house on the corner, and perhaps one of the reasons was that Jackie's elderly mother, Esther, and dad, Lewis, lived down the street. Jackie took care of them.

Since Jackie wouldn't move, Max's parents bought the house next to Jackie and knocked it down to build a swimming pool, basketball court, and waterslide. They created a miniature playground for Jackie's kids and Max. They thought this would keep them from wandering around the neighborhood and playing at the park. It did keep them at home-and it kept all of the neighborhood kids there, too- right in Jackie's yard, where there was always plenty of Kool-Aid, food, and fun.

Since Max was a good kid, his parents didn't have any problem with granting his every wish. Jackie told the story that Max turned seven and spent the weekend at her house; he decided that he just had to attend school with her kids. That Monday morning when she dropped her kids off at school and was driving to drop Max off at his school before heading to work, she noticed that Max was very quiet. She knew that being an only child was very lonely for him, and he didn't want to be alone anymore.

Jackie thought, Poor baby. She wished there was something she could do, but there wasn't. Lil Max's eyes had turned red, and she asked, "What's wrong, baby?"

"I don't want to go to school," said Max.

"You have to go to school so you can be a smart little boy," she said.

"But I want to go to Broward Estates Elementary school with Benjamin and Jeremy," he said.

"Baby, you can't go to school with them. Your parents have you in a nice private school."

"Well, if I can't go with them, then you let them go with me," Max decided.

Tears began to roll down Max's face, and Jackie had trouble trying to drive with tears in her eyes. Jackie broke the silence by taking a deep breath and said, "Oh, boy! Baby, I can't afford to send them to your school."

"Why not?"

"It costs too much, and besides, I'm working to save money for them to go to college. They will have to stay in their school, and you, little boy, will have to stay at yours."

"Well, we'll just see about that," Max said angrily.

Jackie said that she knew that couldn't be Max talking to her like that. He just didn't understand, and in his little mind, if there was a problem, you just fixed it. And if there's something you wanted, you asked for it; undoubtedly a gift he learned from his parents. Jackie smiled and thought, I must say, I have learned a few things from them myself. But then Jackie gave Max a look just to let him know that he had better watch who he was talking to and that she wouldn't tolerate being talked to like that by any child.

When Jackie got home that evening, she got a call from Max's parents asking her if they could pay for private school for her two boys so they could attend school with Max, and it wouldn't cost her a dime. They even told her that they would pay for college tuition. Jackie started crying on the phone. Max's mom had her on speaker, and they were all gathered around the phone. Mr. Thorngill sat waiting to jump in, just in case Jackie needed some convincing. He was a man who didn't have much to say, but when he did, it was a done deal.

Jackie could hear Max in the background crying and saying, "Don't cry, Mama Jackie." At that point, everyone was crying. Jackie had no doubt as to whether or not Mr. Thorngill's eyes were filled with tears. He would often be at the point of tears when he would say to Jackie, 'you must be an incredible person for me to trust you with Max, my most valuable treasure.' Jackie knew that Max's mom's tears weren't because her son called another woman mama; she was happy that someone, this black woman, took such good care of her child and that there was so much love between the two of them. They discussed the matter, and they were not taking no for an answer.

Max's parents always wanted to do more for Jackie, but she would never let them. They had Jackie run the office, so they traveled from time to time. They had earned it. They traveled mostly during the summer when school was out so that Max could travel with them. He would go sometimes. But being a kid, he wanted to play, so he often stayed at Jackie's until they returned from their vacation.

Their entertainment when they were home was having Max tell them all about what he had done with Jackie and her kids. They would sit around and laugh at his stories. Max told them how they were on their way to Broward Meats on a rainy Saturday when Jackie's car broke down. He told his dad how Jackie made them stay in the car while she got out and pushed the car off the road all by herself.

The very next day, a Mercedes dealership delivered a brand-new white Mercedes to Jackie's house. Jackie wouldn't go near it. Max's parents wondered why Jackie was still driving her old car to work. They found out that Jackie wouldn't drive the new car because she thought it was some kind of cruel joke someone was playing on her.

As it stood, anything that would make Mrs. Thorngill's little boy happy, and anything Jackie or her family ever needed, they would have. Mrs. Thorngill was adamant that if an unfortunate accident should take her and her husband, Jackie would be given sole custody of Max. Papers were drawn up and signed, making Jackie executive of their will and giving her sole custody of Max if anything should ever happen to them. The highlight of Mr. Thorngill's day was never some big real estate deal he had closed on; it was rushing home to hear about Max's Day at school and more stories about his weekend at Jackie's.

Jackie had two sons she called Beavis and Butthead. There was only a one-year age difference between Benjamin and Jeremy. Therefore, Jeremy graduated a year after Benjamin. Every time she would call them Beavis and Butthead, she would say, "They aren't really like Beavis and Butthead. I call them Beavis and Butthead because of the practical jokes and pranks they like to play on me."

Whenever Jackie's sons came home for spring break, different women would show up with their suitcases planning to stay at her house with her sons. She would tell them this wasn't a hotel. The women would say that they didn't have money for a hotel. Jackie would then say, "I hope you had sense enough to get a round-trip ticket because you won't be staying here."

"I don't let these lying heifers get away with anything." Jackie said. "Women are sneaky, conniving, and as slick as grease. Oh, they are full of shit, so you can call me ex-lax, cause I'll give them the runs."

Both Benjamin and Jeremy graduated from medical school. Benjamin stayed in Tennessee after graduating from Meharry Medical School, and Jeremy moved back home to be near his mom. He completed his residency at Broward General Medical Center. Jeremy was a trauma surgeon. His office was near the hospital, a graduation gift from Max's parents. They did even better for Ben. To ensure that he wouldn't have to pay to rent office space, they purchased the building for Ben's medical office in Tennessee.

Ben came home for Max's parents' funeral and stayed a week. He made sure he was home at least four times a year; always for New Years, Valentine's Day, Thanksgiving, and Christmas. He joked that his mom was still his only girl, so that was why he was always home for Valentine's Day. The entire office always dropped by Jackie's house for the holidays. Even Broward's sheriffs and Fort Lauderdale police officers dropped by to join in on the festivities. Fort Lauderdale was really the place to be for the holidays.

Once when Ben was home for Christmas, he was teasing Max about Natalie. Ben said that Natalie called him asking him to talk to Max about taking her back.

"Natalie told me that she was pregnant. It isn't mine," said Max.

"I'm a doctor. I can do a DNA test," said Ben.

"You can run all the tests you want. You won't find my DNA." "This mess has lawsuit all over it. Sounds like a matter for the courts."

"Why don't you stick to medicine and leave the legal issues to me?"

"She wants you back, man. Are you taking her back?" Ben asked.

Max replied, "Like my man Jay Z says, I got ninety-nine problems and a bitch ain't one."

Everyone thought it was so funny to hear a white, high-powered attorney talking about Jay Z. Apparently Max thought Jay Z was deep. He had every one of his CDs.

What Ben didn't know was that Natalie had stopped by the office a few times looking for Max when he and Jackie were not there. Everyone hoped she wouldn't show up when Jackie was there. Jackie certainly did not like the woman.

This is one of the reasons why Danielle was finding it hard to stay focus in the meeting. She was critiquing her bosses and doing a mental playback on everything she had heard about each one. Danielle didn't want to date a man with past relationship baggage. She had decided that the next man she dates will be white. However, she wondered if she should take Jess advice and start with her fine white bosses. If she decided to date one of the partners, it would save her from having to find the time and energy of going 'white boy shopping'.

They all continued listening to Ted's excitement about opening the London office and his parents' beautiful country villa where he grew up. He took a deep breath and said, "I'm looking forward to spending time with my parents."

Ted clapped his hands once and said, "I guess it's not true that you can't go home again." He looked at Danielle and asked her to give her report. Danielle glanced at Max and smiled. Max returned the gesture and winked, which caused Danielle's stomach to tighten up in knots. Working closely with him on their case and the stories she'd heard from Jackie about Max made her wonder if he could be the one.

Danielle concluded her report, and the other attorneys took their turns. At the end of the last report, Ted asked that all reports are given to Carmen before heading out to their court appointments. He adjourned the meeting and handed Danielle a file that he wanted her to review for their meeting later that evening.

Chapter 3

The day Natalie stopped by; history repeated itself. The entire office knew that it would not be good for Natalie to show up at the office when Jackie was there. Jackie would do to Natalie what she had done to Mr. Marshall one of Max's clients whom she thought wanted to hurt Max.

Mr. Marshall came to the office screaming about how he didn't want to pay alimony to his wife and that Max had better make sure he didn't. Jackie locked the door so he couldn't get away before she ripped him a new ass. The office staff was afraid for their lives, but not Jackie. Mr. Marshall was a big white man who towered over Jackie and spoke with a Southern accent. He had a lot of money and didn't want to pay alimony. His wife was getting five million, and he was scared she would get more.

Jackie still had his file on her desk. She grabbed the file to verify his contact phone number.

> Jackie: Is your number 954-555-1212?
> Marshall: Yes, it is.
> Jackie: When was the last time you checked your messages?
> Marshall: Couple of days ago. What that got to do with anything?

Jackie: Why don't you check your messages now?
Marshall: I'll do it later.
Jackie: No, you came in here accusing Mr. Thorngill of not doing his job.
Marshall: Did he leave me a message about the alimony? Jackie: You would know if you checked your messages.
Marshall: Do I have to pay alimony?
Jackie: Mr. Thorngill called and left you a message, then asked me to keep calling until I got you on the phone so I could let you know the judge denied your wife's petition for alimony.
Marshall: Boy, that's a relief.
Jackie: Max is a damn good attorney, but in the future, when you need a lawyer, you take your business somewhere else. We don't need your threats or your business.
Marshall: Well, I apologize for the misunderstanding.
Jackie: There's no misunderstanding. You feel you can throw your weight around because of your size. This isn't the place. I need you to leave this building and not come back. Jackie looked Mr.
Marshall in the eye and said very sarcastically: You have a good day, sir, you and your wife.
Marshall: I said I was sorry. I didn't know.
Jackie: Now you do.

Jackie didn't utter another word. She looked as if she were about to explode. She walked over to Helen's desk and placed the keys in her hands. Helen looked at Mr. Marshall, smiled, and said, "Come with me, sir." Mr.

Marshall followed Helen to the front door, where Helen unlocked it to let him out.

Helen returned to find Jackie sitting at her desk very quietly, thumbing through a file. Everyone rushed over to Jackie's desk to ask if she was all right. Ross's secretary, a young Jamaican girl named Charmaine, said, "Miss Jackie, I thought I would wet my pants. I was so scared that big man was gonna step on you and sling you round the room. He could pick you up and body slam you, you know! My God, woman! But you know, even though I was scared, I had your back." They all looked at Charmaine and laughed.

"Why ya'll laughing? I got Jamaican in me. I don't play," Charmaine said.

"Thanks, Charmaine," Jackie said. "I know if something goes down, I can count on you. I know you got my back."

History did repeat itself and this was not a good day for Natalie to stop by for a visit. It was 2:00 p.m., and the office was just about to take its afternoon break when a pregnant Natalie walked in. Max wasn't there; he was still in court. He and Danielle were working on a really big case together-a wrongful death lawsuit. Jackie escorted Natalie to the conference room to wait for Max. After Natalie was seated, Jackie rushed over and locked the door to Max's office; she knew Natalie would try to go through his things to find out what was going on in his life.

After Jackie locked Max's door, she walked over to Helen's- Chad's secretary-desk and looked at the watch on her left wrist. She said, "Helen, watch this. She'll be coming back. She's going to walk over to Max's office to go in as if she runs things. Then she'll ask me for the key to let her in, and then say that because of her condition she needs to be comfortable.

I swear, if that beast tries me today, she better give her soul to God, because her ass belongs to me."

"Don't get yourself in any trouble," said Helen.

"Oh, it's on, and you can believe that. After all the hell she put Max through, she better hope I don't forget that she is pregnant and whoop her ass," Jackie said.

Previous encounters had proved that Natalie could be a real bitch. She had tried to intimidate the staff when she was married to Max. But the way Jackie saw it, Natalie was no longer Mrs. Max Thorngill, and it was open duck season for her ass.

"You just watch," Jackie said. She looked at her watch and began to count, "Five, four, three, two, one."

Helen's eyes widened when she saw Natalie emerge from the conference room and do everything that Jackie had said she would.

Jackie looked at Natalie and said, "Wait right there," before heading out to the lobby.

Natalie slung her hair back, smiling as if she had forced Jackie to do something she didn't want to do. The whole office smiled back because the reason Jackie had gone to the lobby was to make sure there weren't any clients out there and to lock the front door so that no one could walk in while she tore Natalie a new ass. Natalie stood there with her head tilted back as if she was looking down her nose at everyone.

Everyone in the office knew exactly what Jackie had done because they had seen it before. As soon as Jackie returned from locking the front door, Natalie said, "I can't stand around all day waiting on you."

That was when Jackie opened up with both barrels.

"Bitch, you don't need to be standing there at all. I know you didn't think I was going to get keys to let you in Max's office. We don't keep keys in the waiting area. You're really dumb, if that's what you thought. I locked the front door so your ass couldn't get out before I tell you just how I feel about your slimy ass. You no-good, trifling, dirty whore. Just tell me the truth: is your blood type whore positive? What the hell you doing here anyway? Max divorced your ass. Where is that bastard who got you pregnant?"

Natalie responded, "How you know it's not Max's baby?"

"Because he's not that damn stupid," Jackie said. She threw Helen the keys and said, "Here, take these and let this bitch out before I forget she's pregnant."

Just as that was happening, someone began rattling keys at the door to the rear entrance. Max and Danielle walked through the back door and saw Natalie walking toward the entry to the waiting area. Natalie turned and smiled. Max's eyes landed right on her huge belly.

"You're pregnant?"

"Yes," Natalie said softly.

Natalie was obviously expecting more, but all she got from Max was, "I hope you and the father of your baby are very happy."

He put his hand in his pocket and took out his keys to unlock the door to his office as if he knew it was locked. He walked in, locked the door behind him, and closed the blinds, basically telling Natalie to go away.

Perhaps Max acknowledging Natalie's pregnancy was his way of reminding her of how badly he wanted to be a father.

Jackie didn't make the situation any better. When Natalie turned to leave, she yelled, "Don't come back now, ya'll hear? Bitch," Jackie said with a frown. "I can't stand her ass."

Chapter 4

Danielle walked to her office with Jess's ordeal still on her mind. She picked up the phone and called her.

"Hello!" answered Jess.

"What's going on?" Danielle asked. "Where do you want me to start?

"Did you get that Melanie business out of the way?"

"Girl, let me tell you what happened," said Jess. "As soon as I hung up with you this morning, I called Tina to tell her to meet me at the shop. She informed me that Melanie and Slick were planning a trip to the Bahamas. So, I wasn't taking any chances. I arrived at her door at 8:00 a.m. When she answered the door and let me in, I noticed that there were suitcases sitting at the front door. I didn't ask if she was planning a trip. That wasn't my business. I was only concerned about the business I had come there for, and that was her signature on those documents. I wasn't leaving there without it."

"What happened?" Danielle asked.

"I told her that the shipment of weave she had ordered had come in late yesterday, and the supplier said the only way he was leaving the hair would be if I paid the bill, which was $1,500, and provided the owner's signature that the merchandise had been received. Otherwise, the shipment would be returned to the warehouse."

"What did she do? Did she say anything?" '

'Yeah!" said Jess.

"What did she say?"

"She said she didn't have any money. Then she asked, 'Are you paying the whole thing? Do you have my half?'"

"That's what she asked?"

"That's all she wanted to know," said Jess. "She is such a crook.

She never ordered any supplies. I made up the story."

"But how did you know she would sign the papers?" Danielle asked.

"She would have signed anything as long as she thought she was keeping her half of the shop and my money. She thought that if she could trick me into paying for her supplies, she would pull one over on me."

"What a character," said Danielle.

"I stood there looking at her while she signed those papers and was thinking how this bitch had no intentions of coming to the shop to sign them. She was planning on taking a trip with my money and then return from her trip still owning half of the shop."

"Now you know when she gets back from her trip, she's coming for her half of the shop and her $750 worth of weave," Danielle said, laughing.

"If she does, I bet you she won't leave with half of her ass whooped. She's going to leave with a whole ass whooping," Jess promised. They both started laughing.

Danielle's phone beeped. "Jess, let me go. I'll talk to you later. I've got another call."

Danielle switched over to the other line. "Attorney Danielle-"

Before she could finish saying her name, the caller said, "Hello My love, my darling, the light of my life."

Danielle, recognizing Carl Palmer's voice, said, "Oh, I'm your love, your darling, the light of your life?"

"Yes, you are," he said.

"What do you want, Carl?"

"I miss you, baby."

"Sure, you do," said Danielle.

"These women are driving me crazy. They don't want to leave me alone," Carl said, chuckling.

"Sounds like a personal problem to me."

"It could be our problem. What are you doing tonight?"

Danielle laughed really loudly and said, "You shouldn't concern yourself with what I'll be doing tonight."

"I still love you," said Carl.

"Do you really think that I believe you ever loved me? I've come to the conclusion that love is nothing more than a fleeting fancy to you. You always treated me as if you had someone better to do. And tonight, I've got something better to do."

Danielle hung up the phone. After she had placed the phone back on the receiver, she sat at her desk, shaking her head. "He must be out of his damn mind. Thank God the shoe is now on the other foot. I don't give a damn about you anymore. Fucking asshole."

Danielle was furious that Carl would call her and treat her like the damn fool she had been so many times in the past. She felt hurt and used. He was acting as if they were still in a relationship. Danielle thought about how she used to be so in love with him. Now she knew that she would never allow him to place her on the back burner again. She did the only thing she could to calm down: she wrote through her pain. Writing always gave her a release for what she was feeling. She took a notebook from her briefcase and began to write.

Love Is a Fleeting Fancy

My telephone rang, and it was you, calling with that same old mess that's so typical for you. "Hello! My love, my darling, the light of my life." I should have hung up. Yet I replied, "I'm your love, your darling, the light of your life?" "Yes! You are," you said, as if you were joyfully high. "What brought this all on?" I wondered with a relief of gleefulness. Hoping somehow that my prayers had been answered, and that you had come to your senses. I decided to reciprocate, to let you know you're not alone and that I feel the same way. What did I do that for? Because that was all you wanted to hear. To know there was someone sitting and waiting in the wings with a bending ear. Clearly, something is wrong with your thinking. I know it's not me. Perhaps you were struck by lightning or ran into a damn tree. Today you love me. Tomorrow you don't. Maybe next month you'll love me, or maybe you won't. This merry-go-round of your affection is too hard for me to bear. I need to sit and collect my thoughts for a minute. Can someone please get me a chair! No, that's okay, I see the exit door. I'm tired of being treated like a backburner whore.

Danielle sat there fighting back the tears. Max walked in and asked if she wanted to join him for lunch.

"I'm having lunch with Rosario. I guess she's still in court," said Danielle.

"Did you check with Carmen to see if she called? "No! I guess I need to do that."

"I'll ask Carmen," said Max.

As Max walked up, all four of Carmen's phone lines were ringing. One call was from Rosario, calling to check in and leave a message for Danielle that she couldn't make lunch. Max was happy to hear that Rosario wouldn't be able to join them. Another call was from Ted. He was calling Carmen to let her know that he was still at court and that he should return around 3:00 p.m. He asked her to see if the partners were available to meet with him at that time so that they could choose the person who would accompany him to London. Max was not happy that Ted's meeting had interrupted his plans to take Danielle to lunch.

Ted arrived at the office at 2:55 p.m. Chad, Ross, and Max emerged from their offices and followed him into the conference room. Max knew that Ted would tell them he had chosen Danielle to accompany him to London.

Ted began by saying that he had called the meeting to talk about setting up the London office and to hear their thoughts on who would be the best person to assist him with this project. Almost simultaneously they blurted, "Caroline."

Ted smiled and said, "Now that's a collaborative effort. Does anyone want to tell me why you've chosen Caroline?"

"She just got out of a bad relationship, and she can use the trip," said Chad.

"What about you, Max? Why did you choose Caroline?"

"Before she signed on with us, she had her own private law practice," Max said.

"We haven't heard from you, Ross. Why Caroline?" Ted asked.

"I chose Caroline for the obvious reason. I think she has a thing for you, and you're both single."

"You're playing the matchmaker?"

"Man can't live by bread alone," Ross said.

"Well, I think Danielle would be the best choice to travel with me to London, and I can make a very good argument to justify my decision. She has outstanding credentials, unquestionable skills, and a solid work ethic. Are there any disagreements with anything that I've pointed out?"

"There isn't anything that you have said about Danielle that we could disagree on. However," said Max, "you are going to London to set up a new office. You are not going to be in court. We all know she is a great asset to this firm. Therefore, the skills that you pointed out can best be utilized here by helping with all the court cases."

"I've pretty much made up my mind to take Danielle with me, and I plan to make the announcement next week, in the weekly meeting." It was Ted's choice to make, and they had all known that he would choose Danielle. They all secretly wanted to date her and they knew that this was Ted's way of manipulating the playing field to have Danielle all to himself.

However, Max's plan was to let Danielle know that he was interested and thwart Ted's chances. The idea of the two of them alone for two months scared Max. He did not want to lose the chance of making Danielle his. Max knew that if he was going to make his move on Danielle, it had to be before she left for her trip with Ted. *I've got to be a magician to pull this off in two weeks*, thought Max.

Max

Chapter 5

The weekly meeting was about to start, and everyone took their seats. Ted began by saying they had decided that Danielle was their choice to accompany him to London. The partners smiled and nodded their heads in agreement. Max immediately pointed out that he and Danielle had to work late tonight to prepare closing arguments on their case. After all the cases had been discussed, Ted closed the meeting by telling everyone that they were doing a wonderful job and that he expected they would keep up the good work in his absence.

No one was surprised when Ted said, "We're going to be working around the clock, Danielle. I'm going to hold you to your plan."

Danielle smiled and asked, "What plan?"

"Don't you remember?" Ted asked. "You said that the attorney chosen to go to London would have to work hard to complete the project so that they could turn the trip into a vacation."

Max looked at Danielle and said, "Don't you two have too much fun. You might not want to come back."

Danielle said, "I wouldn't worry about that."

Max was worried. He knew Ted wanted Danielle. They all knew. Max saw how Ted watched Danielle and monopolized her time. He even refused to go out on dates with Leslie just so he could spend time with her. He ordered elaborate dinners whenever they worked late.

Unsuspecting Danielle didn't even see what was going on, because Ted was being very subtle. It appeared that Ted, having never been on a date with a black woman before, was somewhat concerned about what his colleagues, family, and friends would think.

Ted was falling in love with Danielle, but he was dragging his feet. He hoped that once they got to London, he would be able to be with her without any outside influences. Ted was concerned that certain people would try to keep them apart. He was in love and playing it safe. Everyone else thought he was afraid of what people would think because Danielle was a black woman. This was far from the truth. He was actually afraid that Danielle might not feel the same about him. Of course, there was one thing he had forgotten about, and that was: *if you snooze you lose.*

The whole office knew Ted was crazy about Danielle. The one thing they didn't know about was that Max planned to make his move on Danielle tonight. He planned to spend the next two weeks marking his territory in hopes that Danielle would not succumb to Ted's charm in London. All he had was two weeks. He knew he had better move quickly. Max didn't care what people thought about his being with a black woman. He had been around black people all his life, and he felt right at home. Max planned to have Danielle and himself be like the song *Me and Mrs. Jones we have a thing going on.* If he could carry out his plan, that is.

Max didn't care that Danielle was black. He adored her. Her dark skin was as smooth as silk. She was everything he wanted in a woman. One of the things he had heard Benjamin and Jeremy repeat quite often was: *the blacker the berry, the sweeter the juice.* But he knew he had to move fast.

Max had set the wheels in motion by telling Ted that he and Danielle needed to work late preparing the closing argument on their case. He knew that was the only way to keep Ted from hogging her time. But Ted was his friend and partner. Therefore, Max knew he had to handle the matter in a way that would hurt no one's feelings. They would chalk it up to the better man winning and walk away.

At the end of the last report, Ted forgot to ask that all reports be given to Carmen before heading out to their court appointments. He adjourned the meeting, but this time he wasn't handing Danielle a file that he wanted her to review. It was Max that would be spending the evening with Danielle.

Later that night after Max and Danielle were done working, they decided to grab a bite. They were both a little hungry. Danielle wanted shrimp-fried rice and spring rolls. Max suggested they go to the Thai spice restaurant on Commercial Boulevard.

"They'll be closed by the time we get there," said Danielle. "Have any suggestions?'

"Why don't we try P. F. Chang's on Sunrise Boulevard, next to the Galleria Mall? It's closer."

"Sure. Let's lock up, and I'll follow you," said Max.

They arrived at the restaurant and were seated in a private booth. The waiter walked up and handed them each a menu. "What can I get you to drink?" he asked.

"I'll have unsweetened iced tea," said Max.

"I'll have the same," Danielle said.

"I'll get your drinks and give you a chance to look at the menu," said the waiter.

"You can take my order now. I already know what I want," said Danielle. "I'll have the shrimp-fried rice and spring rolls."

Max looked at Danielle and smiled. "I'll have the chicken and broccoli with white rice." After the waiter walked away, Max was still looking at Danielle and smiling.

Danielle wanted to know what was so funny. "Why are you smiling?" she asked.

"Is that all you're ordering?"

"That's what I always order when I come here."

Max snickered. "I thought you would have ordered some type of meat."

"For your information, I don't eat meat."

"You don't? I thought all black people ate meat."

"Don't go stereotyping me."

"I'm not," said Max. "I just-"

"Yeah! You just what?" Danielle asked.

"I mean I was surprised, that's all." Max started laughing and said, "I thought that you would have ordered some chicken or ribs."

Danielle looked at Max and said, "No, you did not just go there again. Not all black people eat meat. How would you like it if I pointed out something that is a stereotype for whites?"

"What would that be?" asked Max.

"No," Danielle said, "I'll keep that one to myself."

"Go ahead, I can handle it, I've heard them all." "Well, is it true?"

"Is what true?"

"You know," replied Danielle.

Max, still laughing, said, "You can ask me anything. I'll tell you if it's true."

Danielle said, "I don't want to hurt your feelings." "You can't hurt my feelings. Ask me."

"Okay! If you insist." Now Danielle was laughing. She said, "I heard that white men have small penises. They say it's the size of your pinky."

"Well, little girl, I can assure you my penis is not small, and it is definitely not the size of your little pinky."

Danielle was still laughing as Max continued to defend his manhood.

"It might not be the size of an anaconda, but it is large and very pleasing," said Max.

Danielle looked at Max and said, "Yeah? Tell me about it."

"I don't have to tell you. I can show you," replied Max.

"You show me? I don't think so. Besides, I wouldn't want to be disappointed," said Danielle.

"Sounds like a challenge to me." The food arrived and Max wouldn't stop teasing Danielle. He looked at Danielle's plate and asked, "Where's the meat?"

"You tell me. Where's the beef?"

They were both eating and laughing. Ironically, they continued to laugh and make jokes about the stereotypes of each other's' race. It appears that Max and Danielle were wise enough to see the beauty beyond the surface. It was more than skin deep.

After dinner, Max followed Danielle home to make sure she arrived safely. He walked her to the door and kissed her goodnight. Danielle kissed him back. As they stood there looking at each other, their heart beating fast, neither wanted to rush things. Danielle had vowed that she would not get into a serious relationship anytime soon. Like Danielle, Max had not dated anyone seriously since divorcing Natalie, nor was he looking. They had both been hurt and disappointed by love. This is not what they had planned, but fate knew they needed more than just a casual relationship.

Danielle had thought about dating white men, and here she had one standing right in front of her, and my oh my, was he smoking hot. Max leaned in for another kiss, but Danielle stopped him and said, "You'd better go. We've got court in the morning."

Max smiled, took the key from Danielle's hand, and opened the door. He then handed her back the key, and she said goodnight and walked inside. She didn't close the door. She watched Max as he walked to his car. Max looked back and saw her still standing in the doorway, waving. He decided to throw her a kiss, and then he smiled and drove off.

While Max and Danielle were apart, they couldn't stop thinking about each other. Danielle walked into the bedroom and set her briefcase on the nightstand by the bed. She put in her Pointer Sisters CD, took off her clothes, and grabbed a robe hanging in the bathroom closet. She then pulled a couple of files from her briefcase and sat in the white lounger on the other side of the room to review her cases for the next day. She heard the words, "I want a man with a slow hand," and it made her think about Max.

Danielle finished reviewing her cases and placed the files back into her briefcase. She walked into the bathroom and started running water for her bath. She was just about to take off her robe when her cell phone rang. She turned off the water and walked back to the bedroom. She took her cell phone from her briefcase and answered it.

Danielle: Hello!

Caller: What are you doing?

Danielle: I was about to step into the tub.

Caller: I need to talk to you. Is it all right if I come over? Danielle: Can it wait until tomorrow? I've got to be in court at nine

Caller: No, it can't wait. Let me come over. I promise I'll be brief. Danielle: Okay, come on over. I'll see you when you get here.

Caller: I'm already here.

Danielle: You're here?

Caller: Yes, come to the door.

It was getting late, and all Danielle wanted to do was take a bath and go to bed. She went to the door and opened it. There stood Max. He had gone home and taken a shower but couldn't get Danielle out of his mind. So, he sat on his living room couch and reviewed a few his cases. Then he began writing his opening argument for a murder trial that was scheduled for next month. He got halfway done and realized he was still thinking about Danielle. He put everything away and went to bed, but he couldn't sleep. Max knew his law partners wanted to make a move on Danielle.

After the kiss and having had some quality time with her, he was determined not to lose Danielle to anyone. He reached for the other pillow and held it close to his chest, wishing it were Danielle. Realizing that he couldn't rest, he decided to head back to her house. He contemplated whether she had been kissed by Ted, Chad, or Ross.

Talking to himself while driving, he thought maybe Ted, since they were always working late. Or maybe Juan. Could she have kissed Juan? Juan claimed to be a Latin lover boy. He shook his head. If she had kissed any of them, there was no way she would have kissed him back so passionately. Max had fallen for Danielle, and he had to tell her. He was going to go back to her house and let her know.

Now there he was, back at Danielle's front door, holding his cell phone to his ear.

"Come in," said Danielle. "Would you like a drink?"

"What do you have?" Max asked. Danielle opened the drawer of an English-style white cabinet that stood next to the front door. She took out what looked like a remote control and pressed the button. The entire wall opened up to display the most well- stocked bar imaginable. Max laughed, walked over, and picked up a bottle of whiskey.

"Top shelf," he said. "Can I fix one for you?"

"No, I don't drink that stuff."

"All this and you don't drink?"

"There you go stereotyping again. I said I don't drink that. Courvoisier straight up with a little water on the side is my drink of choice."

They fixed their drinks and sat on the sofa. Danielle sat at one end with her legs crossed, the split on her robe showing off her beautiful, long legs. She took a sip of her drink. Max felt his penis getting hard just looking at her. Danielle looked at Max and asked, "What did you need to talk to me about that was so important it couldn't wait until tomorrow?"

"Can we finish our drinks first?"

She looked at Max and said, "You finish your drink. I need to take my bath before the water gets cold."

"Need any help?" Max asked.

Danielle smiled and said, "No, thanks. I'm good." "I bet you are." said Max.

Danielle went back into her bedroom and closed the door. Max took another sip. His penis was throbbing. He wanted Danielle, and he didn't know how he was going to tell her. He reached into his pants to adjust his penis. Then he took another sip and laid his head back.

Max heard the noise, and he ran to the bedroom door and opened it.

"Are you okay?" he asked.

"Yes, I accidentally banged the handle on the side of the bathtub. I was getting my loofah to scrub my back," replied Danielle.

Max was now standing in the doorway of the bathroom. Danielle looked up and saw him, and she placed her left arm over her breasts as if to hide them. Max stared at Danielle as he walked over, taking the loofah from her hand.

He sat down on the side of her Roman-shaped bathtub and asked, "Why don't you let me do that?"

She leaned forward as Max began to make gentle strokes over her back. After he was done, he laid the loofah on the back of the tub, grabbed the sponge, and began to bathe her. She continued to shield her breasts as he began to stroke the inside of her thighs and legs. She was feeling aroused.

"Let me hold your feet," said Max. He washed one and then the other.

How can I let this happen? she thought. But she knew she didn't want him to stop. She looked at Max and lay back to enjoy every minute of this sensuous bath.

Max moved her arm that was hiding her breasts. She did nothing to stop him and sighed. He ran the sponge in a circular motion over her breast, which caused her vagina to pulsate. She crossed her legs, wondering how a bath could bring her to the point of an orgasm. Max noticed Danielle squeezing her crossed legs even tighter.

He began to slowly and gently stroke her thighs and the top of her vagina, making Danielle's legs open up and allowing him full and complete control. He was right at the spot he wanted to be: between her legs. He rubbed her clitoris three times very softly. He let go of the sponge and stroked her vagina with his hand. Danielle sighed as Max's finger tried to enter her vagina.

Why is her vagina so tight? Max wondered.

He grabbed the sponge that was lying between her thighs and placed it next to the loofah. He grabbed the towel and said, "Come on. Let's get you dry." Max helped Danielle out of the tub. After he dried her off, he wrapped the towel around her and said, "I'll go finish my drink and wait for you."

Danielle put on a black negligee and robe and then went to join Max on the sofa. He reached over and kissed her again and again.

"Don't you want to talk?" Danielle asked.

"We are talking," replied Max.

He ran his hand up her thigh. Danielle's body shook with excitement. She asked herself if this was what it was like to be with a white man. He picked her up and carried her to the bed.

Max took off Danielle's robe and then her negligee. He wanted to undress last so that she could see just what he was working with. Max wanted her to know that not all white men had a small penis, just as not all black men had large ones. He slowly undressed as if he were a stripper. This show was all for her.

Max already knew that Danielle's vagina was tight from the bathtub incident. He thought that if she'd dated someone for a while, she would have had sex, but maybe it wasn't that often. He could see in her eyes that she seemed to be scared by the size of his penis. Max sat on the bed and leaned over to kiss Danielle to assure her that he would be gentle.

Danielle couldn't take her eyes off what was lying halfway down Max's thigh. She was scared that it might hurt. Should she tell him that she was a virgin and had been saving herself, not necessarily for marriage, but for that special man whom she could trust?

"Max," said Danielle. "There's something that I need to tell you about me."

"What is it, baby?" he asked.

"I have never had sex, not even with Carl Palmer. He was busy having sex with other women, and I was busy with my career. You also need to know that I treat my pussy like beachfront property. I never have and I never will rent out a room, allow an overnight stay, or let a man treat it like a vacation spot just because of how much money he has or how he looks. I've got money and plenty of it. I don't need any man to take care of me. So, if you are here just so you can see what it's like to be with a black woman, then I suggest you put your clothes back on and leave my house. We will still be friends, and I promise that I am strong enough to forget this ever happened." Danielle moved her finger down the shaft of Max's penis and said, "You lied to me. This is an anaconda." She laughed.

Danielle grabbed her robe, but Max threw her back on the bed and said, "I listened to you. Now it's your turn to hear me out. I lost my parents three years ago. I divorced my wife, the only woman I have ever had sex with, a year later. So it's been two years since I've had sex. I have been saving myself for someone special. That should tell you something about the kind of man I am. It's not just my body that needs you, Danielle. My heart needs you, too. If only you could look inside my heart and see the sincerity and love that it holds only for you."

His eyes filled with tears as he climbed into bed and kneeled between her legs. He looked at Danielle and pleaded, "Please don't send me away. Let me make love to you.

I promise you won't be disappointed. I see your vagina as a beautiful flower garden. I beg you, please, let me come in. Invite me in to water the flowers in your beautiful garden. When I come in, we shall both dance in the rain."

Max grabbed Danielle's hands, waiting to see if she would allow him to enter into her garden.

Danielle felt Max's penis touching the opening of her vagina.

She began to cry.

"Please don't cry. I can feel your body trembling," said Max. "I promise that I won't hurt you. I'll stay outside until you tell me I can enter."

They were both crying now. Danielle was crying because she thought it would hurt. Max was crying because he didn't know how long he could wait to find the solace he was looking for inside of the warmth of Danielle's body.

Max lay down on top of her to kiss away her tears. He kissed Danielle all over her beautiful black body. He kissed the inside of her thighs, and his tongue moved inside the entrance of her garden. He nibbled her breast softly. Her nipples between his teeth caused her to reach the peak of orgasmic delight. She sighed with pleasure.

Danielle looked at Max and said, "I trust you with my body. I give my body to you to do whatever you want."

Max slowly eased his way into Danielle's garden. He walked slowly through the flowers to find a place just beyond the gate to rest his head. He thought, *What a beautiful garden.* He noticed all of the beautiful flowers that had never been touched by any man. As the caretaker of this garden, he made sure not to bruise or trample any of the flowers. He dared not go any deeper into the garden, so he admired the beautiful flowers in the back from afar. Surely, they would be there the next time he visited.

Max knew that only he had been allowed to enter this beautiful garden to water the flowers. Just the thought of what a privilege he'd been given made him dance for joy. He danced and danced and danced until it began to rain. He watered the entire garden, just as he promised. The flowers were happy that Max came in to water them. They became so excited that they began to cry. The pleasure of the dance had been so intense that tears ran down Max's face.

He looked at Danielle and asked, "How was I for a white boy?"

Danielle looked at him and smiled. There were no words to describe what she had just experienced.

"Let me tell you something," Max said.

"Wait, take it out and then tell me," said Danielle.

"Take what out?"

"Your penis."

Max laughed and said, "Baby, I'm not inside of you. I took it out right after we both reached orgasms."

"It hurts," said Danielle. "It feels like you're still inside of me."

"Look at me. You see--I'm not inside of you."

"Look at you! Are you getting hard again?"

'Sure, looks like it," Max replied.

"Why are you getting hard again? Don't men have a resting period? You need to tell me what I can do, or what you want me to do, that will make that go down. Please, Max, promise you won't put that back in me tonight."

"I promise that I won't penetrate you again unless you tell me I can." Max was laughing so hard he couldn't stop. His heart ached when he saw that Danielle was scared and in pain. When she began to cry, he held her in his arms and said, "Please, baby, don't cry. I am so sorry for laughing. I was thinking about our conversation in the restaurant. That is the real reason I was laughing."

"Yeah, and you didn't come here to talk. You came here to show me how that particular stereotype about white men was a misconception. You started it by telling me that I was supposed to order meat. I never stereotype people. I asked how you would you like it if I stereotyped you. How would I know what a man has in his pants? I've never been with one before tonight. I've never had any kind of sex with anyone until tonight."

Max, thinking about being Danielle's first, began to rub and kiss her thighs.

"No! Max, get off me."

"I'm sorry, Danielle. It's just that thinking about my being your first makes me want you."

"Well, act like I'm a ho and let me go."

Max kissed and nibbled her breast with his teeth. Danielle lay there quietly, as if she were paralyzed. She couldn't move. She forgot all about her pain. Max's sucking and nibbling her breasts seemed to have a calming effect on her. He felt like the king of the jungle, and she was his lioness.

Max climbed on top of her, still nibbling her breasts. He kissed her between her thighs, causing her body to shake with desire. "Danielle, please, baby. Please may I enter in again?"

"Max, you promised."

"I promised that I wouldn't penetrate you unless you told me I could. So, may I enter?"

She felt his hard penis on her thigh. She knew he would be gentle. He had been gentle the first time. His foreplay made her feel so good. How could she refuse?

Max put his hand between Danielle's legs to show her how lubricated she was. "See, baby, the first time was hard because you had never been with a man. The second time will be easier."

"You promise?" Danielle asked.

"Yes, I promise," said Max. "There was uncharted territory in the back of your garden that I didn't get to explore." He nibbled and sucked her breasts until she begged him to make love to her.

While they made love, Danielle asked, "Max, can I get on top?" "Baby, it's too soon. Maybe after a few more times when you're broken in. Then you'll be able to ride me. I think I can control how much goes in if I stay on top. Am I hurting you?"

"No!" Danielle replied.

"Maybe next time, baby. Danielle, it feels so good. Baby, it feels so good. I don't think I can stop," said Max. "Danielle baby, why are you throwing it back on me so hard? I don't want you to get hurt. You don't have to move. You can just lie there."

"Max, I can't stop moving. I don't understand what's happening to me. It feels so good, Max."

"Danielle, please stop."

"Max, I can't."

"Danielle, please. Oh my God! I feel like I'm losing my mind. Baby, please. Oh shit! Don't stop. Don't you ever stop. Marry me, Danielle. Marry me." Max started crying as he reached his climax. They both came together.

They lay in each other's arms until morning. During the night, Max thought about what Ben had always said. According to Ben, there was no such thing as bad pussy. There was only good, better, and best. Max smiled when he thought about how much he loved soul food. He was happy that he had just dined on the best Southern cuisine he had ever tasted. Max finally drifted off to sleep, holding

Danielle and thanking God that he had found someone to love.

Danielle's alarm sounded. She quickly shut it off so it wouldn't disturb Max. She kneeled beside her bed to begin her morning prayer. Max, missing the closeness of Danielle's body next to him, woke to see her like an innocent child kneeling in prayer- nothing like the female lion she portrayed in court. He wanted to make love to her again. However, he knew he had to leave in order to be on time for court. He waited for Danielle to finish praying and kissed her good-bye.

Danielle

Chapter 6

Now that Max had been allowed to water Danielle's garden, his goal was to spend the next two weeks waking up with Danielle in his arms. He promised himself that he would cater to her every need. For the next two weeks, he knew he needed to seal the deal. What could he do to make Danielle fall madly in love with him? Max wondered. He wanted to show Danielle that no man could love her better.

The first week Max and Danielle worked diligently on completing their court case. Max was the lead attorney. Although Danielle had second chair, Max wanted her to deliver the closing arguments. It was pure genius the way she worked the courtroom.

So later that week, Danielle was standing next to the jury, looking directly at them. She moved to the center of the courtroom and said, "Look." She then paused and looked around the courtroom. All eyes were on Danielle, as if they were waiting for her to show them something. Danielle repeated, "Look," and then gestured to the evidence. "When you look at the evidence, pay close attention to the coroner's report. Remember the time of death. Think about the cause of death. The most important task that I am asking you to do is to feel the loss of Mr. and Mrs. Connelly. After you have done all that I asked of you, you have an obligation to make sure that Mr. and Mrs. Connelly are compensated for their loss."

Max and Danielle disagreed as to whether she should refer to the family as my clients or as Mr. and Mrs. Connelly during the closing argument. Danielle stated that they should always refer to a client by name. It was a matter of semantics.

"If I say award my clients, the jury may think that they are doing something for me. But if I say *Mr. and Mrs. Connelly*, they undoubtedly know the person or persons receiving the award," 'You have to make it personal.' said Danielle.

Nearing the end of her closing argument, Danielle looked at Max and walked back over to the jury. "Mr. and Mrs. Connelly are real people. They are real, and what happened to their child is real. Their loss is real. I understand that losing a child can be heart-wrenching. The loss of their child was a senseless and careless death. They are here today to seek justice. What would you want a jury to decide if it were your child? Yes! You are right. That is why you must render a verdict based on the evidence presented in favor of the plaintiff. I rest my case." The jury deliberated for one hour and came back with a verdict in favor of the plaintiffs.

The second week, Max continued to wine and dine Danielle. He was taking her to all of her favorite restaurants. He especially liked cooking dinner to show off his culinary skills. Max and Danielle had spent every night together. He had done everything humanly possible to not just tell her he loved her, but to show her she was special. But two weeks was all he had, and their time together was quickly coming to an end. Max wanted to do something special for Danielle's last night in town. He planned to cook a special dinner and asked that she arrive by 7:00 p.m.

Chapter 7

It was Saturday morning, and Danielle called her friend Jessica to let her know that she would be picking her up around 1:00 p.m. for lunch. Danielle wanted the two of them to spend some time together before she left for her trip in the morning.

Danielle arrived at Jessica's, blew the horn, and Jess walked out to get in the car. "Would you like to go to Cat Fish Dewey on Andrews Ave?"

"That's where we ate lunch last Saturday," said Jess.

"What about Red Lobster on Federal Highway?"

"Now you're talking,"

"I eat there at least three times a week," said Danielle.

"I never get tired of eating seafood."

"Okay! We're going to Red Lobster."

"I've been meaning to ask you something," said Jess.

"Ask me what?"

"Where did you and Max go for dinner last night?"

"He took me to Mango's on Las Olas for dinner and dancing.

Last Friday night he took me to the Olive Garden."

"Where did you go the night before?"

"We didn't go out. He cooked me dinner," said Danielle.

"Well, what night were the two of you on his boat?"

"That would have been last Sunday. We had dinner at Houston's in Pompano on Atlantic Boulevard," said Danielle. "What's with all these questions?"

"Tina told me she saw you at J. Alexander's on Federal Highway with a white man."

"If she saw me it had to be Tuesday, because on Wednesday Max ordered Italian food from a restaurant called Zuccarelli's."

"Oh my God! I absolutely love their vegetarian lasagna," said Jess.

"You're right—their vegetarian lasagna is the best! But every dish I've tried was amazing," said Danielle.

"By the way, how does Max feel about your going out of town with Ted?"

"I think he has some reservations about my going, but he knows that it's just work. I've noticed that Max has been in a strange mood and acting really secretive these last few days. He has been planning this special dinner for us all week. He constantly reminds me not to be late."

"Well, I wouldn't worry about it if I were you. Just go with the flow," said Jess.

They arrived at Red Lobster and went inside. The hostess walked up and asked where they wanted to be seated.

"It doesn't matter," said Jess.

Danielle liked sitting at the table in the corner on the south side, right next to the window that faced Federal Highway, but she decided not to say anything.

As they sat waiting for the waiter to take their orders, Jess warned Danielle about what to expect when dating a white man. "You know that when people see you with a white man, they are going to be putting you down," said Jess.

"What do mean putting me down?"

"Well, for starters," Jess said, "they're gonna say that you're successful and black, and why couldn't you find a black man? I hate to break it to you like this, but you know black men will be the first to take offense."

"Girl, don't make me curse. Let's just lay it all on the table. Black men have been putting black women down for years. Let me just tell you about some of the things that I have heard from black women," said Danielle. "Black men always tell them why they date white women or any other woman who's not black. They can't be with black women because we are too bossy, too pushy, too demanding, and too argumentative. Oh, and the main one is we don't know how to please them in bed. Can you believe that shit?"

"Yeah," Jess said, snickering, "I've heard a few myself. Didn't you hear the one about how we don't know how to give good head?"

"The belief is that white women are dating black men because they've got large penises. Well, I think it's time black women have a voice and start speaking out. Maybe they need to hear a different take as to why black men are dating white women."

"What is your take on the subject?" asked Jess.

"I don't see jungle fever as the culprit. I think that they are suffering from the forty acres and a mule syndrome."

"What kind of syndrome?" asked Jess.

"Have you ever noticed that with some black men it doesn't matter how rich or successful they become, they don't feel that they have truly made it to the top until they have a white woman on their arm? Some even leave the black women who helped them get to the top for the single white female. You really can't blame the white woman—she is just being smart. The white man promised the black man forty acres and a mule. This debt was never paid. Therefore, there is a possibility that the mindset is you did me wrong and you still owe me. Now, I'll do something that I know you really don't like and date your white women."

"I never looked at it like that. You're probably right. It's the same scenario over and over, and it's not with only the athletes," said Jess.

"If black men are suffering from the forty acres and a mule syndrome, you can't blame them for choosing to be with a white woman."

"I guess we are going to have to join them and start dating white men. I have always heard that an even swap ain't no swindle. And what's good for the goose is good for the gander," said Jess.

"I honestly feel that the heart does whatever it wants. You can't control with whom you fall in love. Everyone has a right to love and be with whomever they choose. We need to respect each other. The bottom line is we are all just squirrels in the world, trying to get a nut," Danielle said.

"I hear that loud and clear. I agree with you 100 percent. But there is one factor that all men have in common."

"What factor would that be?" Danielle asked.

"All men suffer from C.R.S."

"What is C.R.S?" asked Danielle.

"They can't remember shit," Jess replied. "Think about it. Anytime you confront a man about something he did or didn't do, his reply is, 'I don't know what you're talking about. I don't remember.'

"Well, that's why I make it a habit to never confront any man. You never ask questions when you already know the answers. For instance, when you catch your man cheating, you do not ask, 'What are you doing with her? Why didn't you call me? Who do you want? Do you love me?"

"He's only going to lie," said Jess.

"When you ask these questions, you may not get the answers you want, and the situation could prove to be very embarrassing. The fact is you already know the answers."

"We can't put it all on the men. Some women are lying cheats, too. What can an honest person do?" asked Jess.

"Do what I do and pray the Serenity Prayer.

'God grant me the serenity
to accept the things
that I cannot change.
The courage to change
the things that I can.
And the wisdom
to know the difference.'

"After I pray, I have peace in knowing that things are the way they should be. Otherwise, they would be different. What we need is someone to teach our black men how to love and treat black women. Most black men are raised by black women in single-family homes. Our men need male role models. Someone like Tom Joyner, Steve Harvey or Denzel Washington would be my choice," Danielle said.

"Steve Harvey?" Jess asked in surprise.

"Yes, Steve Harvey would be the perfect man for the job."

"Girl, I can just see Steve teaching a class on relationships. He would probably tell them the pot can't talk about the kettle. I have no idea what he would say about an interracial couple."

"Steve keeps it real. He might tell them to just be happy."

"So many black women like Tina, Brenda, and Anne are unhappy in their relationships. Do you remember what Tina said in the book reading?"

"No, I don't remember," said Danielle.

"She said that her husband is always laughing and soft-spoken with his co-workers and friends. But the moment he gets home, he's cursing out her and the kids. He is cursing and fussing from the time he walks in until the time he showers and leaves."

"You see that shit. That dirty bastard has another woman. He starts an argument just so he can leave, hoping that she is still upset when he returns. This will keep her from asking him where he has been all night. He makes sure that everybody in the house is glad he's gone, because when he is home, all he does is curse and fuss. Does he ever spend any quality time with her and the kids?" asked Danielle.

"Not to my knowledge," replied Jess.

"That's sad."

"Almost all the women had something to say about how their men treat them," Jess said.

"I didn't hear Brenda say anything."

"Brenda is the one who said all her husband does when he is home is rub on that car of his."

"I thought Anne made that statement."

"No, Anne said these men love their rides better than they love us. Anne's husband took money from their savings account to buy rims for his truck."

"Our black men need help. Someone has to step up to the plate and teach them."

"Maybe Steve will write another book."

"He should. He wrote an excellent book titled *Act Like a Lady, Think Like a Man*. I think he should write a book that teaches black men to be fathers, husbands, and lovers. I honestly think he is the best man for the job."

"You might be right," said Jess.

"If women of all races stood up and announced what it is we want, you just might hear, 'We want a man with a slow hand, a lover with an easy touch. Someone who will spend some time, not come and go in a heated rush. We want slow moves and slow grooves all night long. Big ain't always better."

"Mmmmm, listen to you, Miss Thang," Jess said, laughing.

"Well! I'm just saying," said Danielle.

"But, if you're gonna do the Pointer Sisters, you can't talk it through." Jess pulled out her iPhone, scrolled down to the music, and pressed the play button. She adjusted the volume on her blue tooth and then looked at Danielle and said, "You don't talk a Pointer Sisters song; you have to sing it."

Jess started to bounce and move to the beat. They both began to sing along, and they sang until the song was finished.

"Now that was fun," said Danielle.

"Yeah, it was. But we always have fun when we get together," said Jess.

"We are not fair-weather friends," said Danielle.

"What is a fair-weather friend?" Jess asked.

"A friend you only see when they have storms in their life. But when you are having rainy days and darks clouds, they are nowhere to be found. They only come around when it's fair weather."

"I know you have always had my back. I have never given you any money. You give me money all the time. I can always count on you not to put me down and act as if you are better than me. I don't have to worry about your showing off your intelligence by using big words that I don't understand."

"Let me explain something to you, Jess. You can always tell the meaning of a word by the words around it."

"What do mean?"

"Do you know what imperative means?"

"No."

"I'll use the word in a sentence, and you tell me what it means."

"Okay, go ahead."

"Listen, Jessica, it is absolutely imperative that I be at the airport at 6:00 a.m. because my flight leaves at 8:00 a.m. and I don't want to miss it."

"Girl, stop worrying. I'll be at your house at 5:00 a.m."

"You'd better be," said Danielle. 'But I want you to tell me what imperative means. I just used it in sentence.'

"Oh, sorry, I wasn't listening."

"You were listening, but you were not paying attention. I said it's imperative that you have me at the airport at 6:00 a.m. because I don't want to miss my flight," repeated

Danielle. 'Now tell me what imperative means by the words around it.'

"It means important. It's important that you be at the airport at that time." Jess laughed. "It also means necessary."

"You see how smart you are? So don't let people treat you as if you're stupid. You can always infer what a word means by what is being said."

"Okay, now I got it. I can tell that the word infer means to understand. So, I infer that you are paying for lunch since you are the one who invited me," said Jess. 'Plus, you are the one with all the money.'

"Stop talking as if you don't have money. You're not poor," said Danielle.

"I got a little money," said Jess. "But I don't have it like you. You're rich."

"Yes, I'm rich now, but I can remember, as my mama used to say, when we were both living on the hog." Danielle laughed and made a gesture to the waiter to bring the check.

While they were waiting on the check, Jessica asked, "What are you going to do, being in London for two long months with Ted O'Reilly?"

"Work," answered Danielle.

"Umm hmm, how come every time I call, when you're working late it's not Max you are working late with; it's Ted?"

"I work late on cases with all the partners and with the other associate attorneys too," said Danielle.

"I work late with all the partners and the associate attorneys too," said Jess, mimicking Danielle. 'Dani, don't be stupid or act as if you don't know that Mr. Fine-ass Ted doesn't have the hots for you. The two of you are going to be in London alone for two long months, and you honestly think nothing will happen? I've seen the two of you together in crowds. Every office party that you have invited me to, he's waltzing you around the room introducing you to all of his friends and the other lawyers, telling them how beautiful you are and that you're such a brilliant attorney. He tells the story at every party about how you kicked his ass in court on that murder trial. He's always parading you around to let them all know that the black woman on his arm is not just a pretty face, but she's a high-powered attorney, and he's proud to have you by his side.'

"But he's dating Leslie," said Danielle. 'Besides, I think you're reading too much into all of this. It's just office politics. He's just being nice, that's all.'

"Nice my ass," said Jess. 'I've watched the two of you when you're together, and I can just imagine how it will be if you two are alone in London. I don't doubt for one minute that the two of you will be knocking boots.'

"We're going to be working," said Danielle. 'I have made my choice. I am dating Max now.'

"Well, you know what they say: when you can't be with the one you love, you love the one you're with."

Danielle looked puzzled. "Stop it, Jess!"

"No, you stop it," snapped Jess. "You're deluding yourself if you think that that white man doesn't want you."

"You said the key word, Jess. Want! I don't want any man to just want me. I want to be loved. And I know that Max loves me."

"Ted is going to be in love with you too. Just as soon as you give him some of that good ole stuff."

"Where's the waiter?" asked Danielle.

"Look who's changing the subject."

"I'm doing no such thing. I had lunch with you, and this evening I'm spending the night with Max before I leave for London in the morning.

"Go ahead and say it. I'm going on vacation with Ted, my fine—ass white boss."

"Damn, I just wish it was me," Jess said with a sigh. "I'll screw that white boy's socks off." She laughed.

"No, you wouldn't," said Danielle.

"Oh, yes, I would," said Jess. "I'll screw him all night long. I'll ride him like a horse, milk him like a cow, and suck him dry. Not necessarily in that order."

"Where is that waiter?" Danielle asked again.

The waiter came over, placed the check on the table, and walked away. Danielle looked at the bill and then reached into her purse and placed a fifty-dollar bill on the table.

The waiter hadn't brought their check earlier because he didn't want them to leave. He was nearby holding the check and enjoying listening to their conversation about white men. He, being white, loved what he was hearing. He kept running to the kitchen to tell everyone about the conversation between this pretty black female lawyer and her friend.

The waiter heard Jess say again, "I'll fuck his socks off."

"Sure, you would, Santa Claus," Danielle said, laughing.

"Finally. Thank you, thank you," said Jess. She put her hand to her chest, as if to take a bow, and then said, "I finally get my recognition as a true Santa."

"You are one sick ass, that's what you are."

"And you, my dear, will get fucked when you go to London," said Jess. "I tell you what: let's make a bet."

"What kind of bet?" asked Danielle.

"Come on, humor me, Dani."

Danielle chuckled. "Ted said the same thing to me."

"Damn what Ted said to you. I'm trying to tell you what that fine-ass white man plans on putting in you. But first, let me teach you three words, seeing how you taught me two new words for the day."

"What three words do you want to teach me?"

"Lack of nookie," replied Jess.

"Well, I know the term lack of, but what is nookie?"

"Don't be so fast. Let me explain what I mean when I say lack of nookie," Jess said. "Now you know you're going to London for two long months and leaving your fine white boyfriend you've been having sex with here. According to you, while you're in London you're going to be working, and not once are you going to have sex with Ted. Therefore, you will be going without sex. In other words, you won't be getting any. To put it mildly, you should be suffering from lack of nookie. But you won't, because I'm willing to bet you that you, my dear, beautiful friend, will be screwed more times than you can count. Lack of nookie will be the least of your worries." Jess laughed.

Danielle wasn't laughing; now she was worried. What if Jess was right and Ted really did like her? She was wondering how to get out of going on this trip. Should she even get on the plane? Danielle was scared that she might hurt Max. Her stomach tightened into knots. She knew she wouldn't approach Ted. But what if he came on to her? Could she resist his charm, and did she even want to? Jess had opened her eyes, and she didn't like thinking about the possibility of what could happen. Her flight was scheduled to leave in the morning, and it was too late to back out now.

"So, do we have a bet?" Jess asked.

The waiter walked up, and Danielle handed him the check and told him to keep the change.

Jess stood up and said, "Wait for me. I need to run to the ladies' room."

The waiter looked at Danielle and whispered, "I don't want to lose my job, but I overheard some of your conversation. Would you please forgive me for speaking to you on a personal level?"

"Go ahead and say whatever is on your mind. My friend Jessica just did."

"Well, if I were you, I wouldn't take that bet."

"You wouldn't?"

"Not in a million years. One thing is for sure: if your friend is correct about your boss introducing you to all his friends, then he will come on to you. Allow me to be blunt, if I may. You need to get to know both men before you decide to settle for either of them. Who knows, you might like the one you're traveling to London with better."

"Is that your advice?" Danielle asked.

"My advice is to have some fun and enjoy life. You're young and beautiful."

Danielle smiled and said, "Thank you. By the way, don't worry; you're not in any trouble."

Jess returned and looked at Danielle and the waiter's smiling at each other. As the waiter walked away, she said, "Girl, I can't leave you alone for a minute without your having some white man hitting on you."

"He was just keeping me company while you were gone. Oh, and about your bet-I'm not making any bet with you about Ted. I love Max, and if Ted does come on to me in London, I'll deal with it. And just for the record, I live a full life, and I'm happy. I never have and I never will suffer from lack of nookie, lack of sex, lack of anything. I am my own woman, and as I have told you so many times, whatever I do with any man, black or white, will be on my terms. I'm dating Max and I love him, but he hasn't put a ring on my finger."

Jess looked shocked and asked, "What did you and that waiter talk about?"

"Girl, get your purse, and let's get out of here. I need to go to Macy's at the Broward Mall and pick up a few things for my trip."

"I bet you do," said Jess as they walked out of the restaurant.

Jessica

Chapter 8

On their way to the Broward Mall, Danielle thought about how people were so quick to judge. She wondered what kind of things people would say or the looks she and Max would get when people saw them together as a couple. She decided that she really didn't give a damn. She knew she loved Max and that he loved her. They simply enjoyed being together.

Danielle glanced over at Jess and said, "You know what, Jess? I was just thinking about my relationship with Max. The man I love just happens to be a white man, and he treats me like a princess. I have made my choice, and I have decided that I'm living my life and doing whatever the hell I want with my life. There is nothing wrong with dating outside of your race. People are people. You can't help with whom you fall in love. Honestly speaking, an intelligent person wouldn't have a problem seeing two people of a different race together. A person of intelligence would know and see that two people get together because of how they make each other feel, not because of the color of their skin. Jess, let me ask you a question. Has any white person ever been really nice to you?"

"Yeah, I meet nice white people all the time. What are you getting at, Danielle?" Jess asked.

"I need to know if there was ever a black person who could have been there for you or help you, but didn't seem to care about your dilemma. Just when you thought all was lost and there was no help in sight, someone of another race came to your rescue. It didn't necessarily have to be a white person. That person could be Asian or Hispanic."

They turned into the Broward Mall and parked in front of Macy's. But because they were still engrossed in conversation, they sat there talking.

"I see what you're getting at here," said Jess. "When I was attending cosmetology school with these two black girls who lived in my building, Frankie and Cassie, they rode with me every day, and I never charged them a dime. When my car broke down, Cassie bought a car and wouldn't even give me a ride. One day I was leaving early to catch my bus because we were having finals, and it began to rain. I ran back to the building entrance. The two them came out of the building, ran past me, got into the car, and drove off. The Spanish lady who lived on the first floor, Maria, was sitting in her favorite spot near her window watching the whole time. Maria walked up to me with her keys in her hand, an umbrella, and two raincoats. She said, 'Come on, my chica. Tell me how to get to your school.' I began to cry.

"On the drive, Maria talked and I listened. She told me the story of how she came to Florida on the Mariel boatlift.

She answered a want ad in the Miami Herald for a housekeeper to work in Fort Lauderdale. She was all alone in the world, so she took the job, and when the kids in that family got older, they didn't need her as a live-in housekeeper anymore. She moved into our building, in that same apartment. Maria ended up buying the building from this white couple with the money given to her by the family she worked for and with money she had saved.

"None of us are of the same race. We were just people helping one another. I was still sobbing until she said, 'Don't cry. Mark my word, the day is coming when those two little cockroaches will show up at your door with their hands out. When they come around needing you, I want you to help them. That will be your way of keeping them under your feet.' Ever since that day, I have been going by checking in on her. Sometimes we go for a walk in the park so she can get out of the apartment. I bring her dinner and carry her to her doctor appointments. I usually leave work and run her errands."

"Is that the person you would always order an extra dinner for?" asked Danielle.

"Yeah."

"Girl, I thought you were feeding some man, or maybe you had gotten yourself a cat," Danielle said, laughing.

"Me and a cat. Now you got jokes," said Jess. "I left work Monday to take Maria to what I thought was a doctor's appointment. But she had me take her to her attorney's office."

"Why would she need to see an attorney?" Danielle asked.

"She had made out her will, and her attorney needed her signature. She is leaving me everything she owns, including the apartment building."

"Jess, I'm so happy for you," said Danielle.

"Why didn't you call and tell me?"

"I called several times, and you were in court."

"That must make you very happy."

"No, I feel sad," said Jess.

"Why would you be sad about someone loving you so much that they would leave you all of their worldly possessions?" asked Danielle.

"Because for me to take possession of everything she owns would mean that I would no longer have her in my life, and that makes me sad," said Jess.

"I see that Maria is the mother you never had, and she loves you."

"Yes, Maria does love me, but I often think about the bitch who gave birth to me." She just turned her back on me and walked away. When my grandmother died, I needed her.

"Please don't dwell on it Jess. The last time we had a conversation about your mother it ended with both of us crying."

"I'm not sad Dani. I was blessed to be raised by my grandmother. When she died, the state sent me to live with my cousin in New York."

"They really rained on our parade. We were getting ready to go to the twelfth grade and couldn't wait to be high school seniors," said Danielle.

"Yeah, we were looking forward to prom night. We had already designed our prom dresses and picked out our hairstyles." Jess said.

"The state just took you away. They wouldn't let you stay with me and my mom." said Danielle.

"One of the saddest days of my life was hearing the state say that I had to live with family. What a damn joke."

"Jess, did something happen to you while you were in New York?" Danielle asked.

"Please don't remind me of that hell. I never told you because I didn't want to talk about what happened to me," Jess said. 'Now that I am older, I guess I can tell you what happened. Do you remember the movie *Training Day* when Denzel Washington said, "King Kong ain't got nothing on me?" Jess asked.

"Yeah, I remember that scene," said Danielle.

"Well, let me tell you, girl, Cinderella ain't got nothing on me," said Jess. 'My cousin made me drop out of school and get a job. I did all the cooking, cleaning, and laundry for her, her kids, and that nasty boyfriend of hers. She caught him looking at me and accused me of trying to steal her man. She threatened to throw me out on the streets."

"You've got to be kidding," said Danielle.

"Not on your life," said Jess. "Later that night, I heard them arguing, and he told her he would leave and never come back unless she let him have sex with me, and that low-down, dirty bitch agreed to let him if he didn't leave her.

"I grabbed my shoes and coat and climbed out the window onto the fire escape. I left there and never looked back.

"I know sometimes we joke around about my not dating, but, Dani, that ordeal made me terrified of men. I often cry myself to sleep because I want to be with a man, but I just can't seem to move past that traumatizing night."

"Come on, Jess, are you trying to tell me that you've never had sex?" Danielle asked. "Are you a virgin?"

"Not for long, I hope," said Jess. "I met this doctor named Jeremy at Starbuck's about a month ago, and we always chat while we're waiting on our coffee."

"You said his name is Jeremy, and he's a doctor?"

"Why? Do you know him?" Jess asked. "Please don't tell me that you dated him."

"No, I never dated him," replied Danielle.

"How do you know him?"

"If he's the same person, I think I know his mother," said Danielle.

"Look at me! Who am I kidding?" Jess said. "There's no way he could ever fall for someone like me when he's got a slew of beautiful female doctors and nurses."

"Don't make me curse. You look like Beyonce's twin," said Danielle. "You just need to stop dressing so homely.

You make yourself look like an old woman. I'm taking you into this store and buying you a new wardrobe."

"My God! We came here to shop, and we are still sitting in the car talking."

"How long have we been out here?" Danielle asked.

"I'm not sure, so come on. Let's go shopping," said Jess.

"Wait, finish telling me what happened to you when you were in New York."

"I'll finish telling you if you take me to the Saw Grass Mall. There's this sexy red dress I would love to get just in case Jeremy asks me out for a date. We can come back to Macy's after," said Jess.

"Sure, just get back to the story and finish telling me what happened."

"Wait, you're not going to ask me how much the dress costs?" Jess asked.

"No," said Danielle. "Don't you want it?"

"Yes, I really want that dress."

"Then that's all I need to know," said Danielle.

"Maybe you can get one just like it."

"No, I can't," Danielle said, laughing. "You are not going to have us looking like the damn Bobbsey twins. Your ass must be traumatized. Finish telling the story."

"I shouldn't tell you anything," said Jess. "You're probably planning on going to New York to do something to my cousin's boyfriend and coming back in time for your trip. I know you. I know how your mind works. You call me crazy. I'm funny crazy. You're really the one who's scary crazy."

"Did he do anything to hurt you?" Danielle asked.

"No," said Jess.

"Well, you don't have anything to worry about. God will punish him," said Danielle.

"If anyone should ever harm me, I wouldn't tell you," said Jess. I don't want you getting into any trouble. Why do you think I dealt with Melanie on getting those papers signed? You might as well admit it-you're crazy. I bet you couldn't work thinking about what you were going to do to Melanie and Slick. I haven't forgotten about what you did to those girls who ganged up on me when we were in the tenth grade."

"See, you don't know the whole story," said Danielle. "Let me just enlighten you as to what really went down. Your grandmother came over and told my mother about what those three girls did to you, and that you were in the hospital. Your granny didn't want me to go to school because they were planning on getting me next. They said it was because we thought we were cute.

"My mama thanked your granny for telling her and said, 'Danielle will not be missing school for nobody, and she damn sho ain't running.' Mama sat me down and had a long talk with me. She said, 'I ain't never ran from a bitch, and I ain't going to pick today to start running. And neither are you.' She told me that if anybody ever threatened to whoop your ass, you tell them, 'You got to bring ass to get ass, you can't whoop ass long distance. You tell them they got to bring it to get it.' She promised me one thing."

"What was that?" Jess asked, laughing.

"She promised me that if I let those girls beat my ass, I had another ass whooping coming when I got home. Therefore, I didn't have a choice. Nobody gave me a choice. I had to fight, and she taught me how that night. She made me stand up, and she showed me what to do. She said, 'Find something solid that you can put your back against so nobody can get behind you. When you got your back against a wall, stand your ground, and you'd better wear their asses out.' She said she wasn't getting in it until she had to. Then she said some crazy mess I'll never forget."

"What did she say?" Jess asked.

"Two peas in a bucket, all ain't for it, mother fuck it."

"Now, that's crazy," said Jess.

They were at the stoplight waiting to turn into the Saw Grass Mall. Danielle didn't realize the light had changed, and the car behind them blew its horn. They were still laughing.

"Girl, Pauline was a mess," Danielle said. "I can hear her now: 'If you run from them today, they'll have you running and hiding from them every day. Don't you let anyone bully you.' She kept saying it over and over. 'Don't be afraid of a bully. You'd better stand your ground and fight back.' Girl, my mama fussed and cursed all night. I couldn't get any sleep."

"Why didn't you tell her you needed to get to sleep?" Jess asked.

"Why didn't you bring your ass home from the hospital and come and tell her for me?" Danielle asked.

"No, I'm glad you didn't do that. We both would have been in the hospital," Jess said, laughing.

"I kept hearing over and over, 'You'd better not start a fight, but you damn sure better finish it. Don't let me find out that you didn't fight back."

"You know, I remember all those one-line sayings of your mom. Mrs. Pauline, what a character," said Jess. "When I got back to Florida and found out she had passed, it hurt so bad because I knew you must have been devastated. She was all you had."

"Like you and your grandmother—she was all you had."

"Now we are all we've got. Just the two of us," said Jess.

Danielle looked over at Jess and said, "You think you're slick. You deliberately changed the subject. You are avoiding telling me about New York. But we are not getting out of this car until you finish telling me what happened. I know you want that dress, so start talking."

"Please! I am not worrying about that dress. I know you're going to buy it for me."

"Don't count on it," said Danielle.

"You're not going to rest until you get me that dress. I know you. Anything that you think I want or need, you will not rest until you have gotten it for me. So who are you kidding?" Jess asked.

"You think you're slick. Your name should have been Slick. Slick ass," said Danielle.

"You keep changing the subject."

"Dani, promise me that you will never go to New York and do anything to Reese and get yourself in trouble, and then I'll tell you."

"I promise. Now finish telling me what happened."

"I will tell you," said Jess, "just as soon as we get back to the car."

"Okay! Let's go get this dress you want."

They went into the mall, and Danielle bought Jess the sexy red dress that she wanted. After they were done, they got into the car and headed back to the Broward Mall.

"Okay! Jess, finish telling me about what happened to you while you were in New York," said Danielle.

"Well, I had the keys to the restaurant where I worked because I had to open up the restaurant every morning for the breakfast crowd. This all happened on a Wednesday night, and I didn't have a place where I could go to be safe. So, I had to sleep at the restaurant that night. I was planning to wait until I got my check on Friday, but Reese came to the restaurant looking for me. He was beating on the door until these two cops showed up and thought that he was trying to break into the building. They took him to jail.

"I was asleep in one of the booths. He had to have seen my feet sticking out or something. He acted as if he knew

I was in there. He was trying to get to me. I curled up into a fetal position and waited until they were gone.

"I was so afraid that he would come back for me that I crawled to the kitchen, grabbed a knife, and slept on the kitchen floor in the corner. I knew that I couldn't work there anymore. I had to get my check and leave, or my cousin would come in and say that she needed my check early to pay the rent and cash it, like she did every week.

"As soon as Mr. Johnson and his wife came in that morning, I told them that I needed my check and explained to them what happened. I was crying and begging them to please give me my check and help me get back to Florida. Mr. Johnson wrote me a check. But Mrs. Johnson tore up the check and gave me cash. Girl, she even took me to the bus station and paid for the ticket. She told me to keep the money that I earned so that I could buy food to eat.

"Before we left for the station, Mr. Johnson wanted to know what to tell my cousin when she came to pick up my check. Mrs. Johnson turned around and gave him this look and said, 'You'd better tell that hooker that I took this child to the police station. That should keep her trifling butt away from here.'

"Girl, I was trying to make it to your mama's house. That's when I first found out your mom had passed away, and you were at Harvard studying law. I didn't have anywhere to go, so I stayed at a women's shelter."

"The same year my mother passed, I had gone to New York looking for you on spring break," said Danielle. "I tried to find you using the address from one of your old letters. When I arrived at your cousin's house, a little girl around nine or ten answered the door. She was wearing only her panties. There was a man with gold on his two front teeth sitting on the sofa. The little girl looked scared. 'Is Jessica here?' I asked. She shook her head and said no very softly.

"The man jumped up and said, 'Who is that looking for Jessica?' He came to the door and asked, 'Do you want to come in?' 'No, thank you,' I said. 'I'm looking for Jessica. Is she here?' 'Nah, she ain't here. She ran away. I believe she went back to Florida. She should have stayed here. I would have taken good care of her,' he said, smiling as he looked back at the little girl, who was now sitting on the sofa. I heard a woman's voice yell out from one of the rooms. 'Are you finished out there?' 'No!' he said. 'I need another hour.' I didn't know what was going on in there. But the one thing I did know, I didn't want any part of it.

"I wrote a letter to Mrs. Sara, your grandmother's friend, asking her to find you and have you call me. I lived off campus in my own apartment. I wanted us to be roommates. We had planned to graduate from high school together. Our graduation and prom night were taken from us; I thought we could at least graduate from college together. I was writing and sending you checks," said Danielle.

Jess looked at Danielle and laughed. "Mrs. Sara was my second choice when I got back here. The only people who were staying in her house were her cracked-out grandchildren and their crack friends. Mrs. Sara had been placed in a nursing home."

"I don't believe this," Danielle said angrily.

"Believe what? What's wrong?" Jess asked.

"If you never got all those letters and the money I sent you, who got them? Where are they?" Danielle asked. "No one but you should have opened and read those letters."

"We can easily find out who cashed the checks."

"I don't give a damn about the checks. They can keep the money. But those letters contained information about my assumed name and what I was doing in college to make money; information that I was making you, and only you, privy to about me."

"Is that what you meant when you said you told me about your assumed name?" Jess asked.

"Yes, that is exactly what I meant. They took something from me, and I am hurt and pissed off. I am tired of people stealing and taking what belongs to me," said Danielle. "That's why I had taken an apartment off campus. My roommate and her friends would often help themselves to all of my book reports, term papers, poems, and screenplays. I walked into the dorm room one day after I had left the library and caught my roommate's boyfriend downloading my files onto his flash drive. When I asked him why was he using my computer, he said that he was just playing a game.

"One semester I took a creative writing course, and I wrote a play called Girls' Night Out. The dumb bastards didn't even change the storyline. They only changed the first word of the screenplay. The one thing they forgot was that I could prove that it was my work because it was a true story. The characters were real. I put a twist on it and threw something extra in that they wouldn't know about just to make it interesting.

"Everything I write has some truth in it. That's how you could recognize and tell that it's my work. Professor Atkins's and Professor Plumb's handwritten notes are all over my plays. I had several rewrites on that particular play. The story was about us. Do you remember when we worked during the summer for the Broward Employment and Training Administration? We had all planned to go to Port Everglades to that club called Pleasure's.

"You and I went to a thrift store downtown near the governmental center off Andrews Avenue. You bought a cute little black dress to wear that night. I wrote about everything that happened. You were either the main character or the supporting character in almost everything I wrote."

"You know what, Dani? You really do need to go away for a while and just have some fun. It has to hurt when someone steals from you."

"That's not all that has been taken from me. Do you remember when we were in the eleventh grade and I worked that year for the Broward Juvenile Detention

Center? I had to complete my community hours in order to graduate high school. I came home and told you how we had CPR training that day and everybody had to practice on this dummy."

"Yeah, I remember," said Jess.

"I told them that I was not putting my mouth on that dummy."

"You always have been a clean freak," Jess said, laughing.

"Anyway, I thought about it and decided there had to be something I could use to avoid catching some kind of disease. So I sat on my bed that night and made a prototype that could be used to administer mouth-to-mouth resuscitation. I took it to a patent attorney's office on Broward Boulevard, and he never called me back. I kept calling him. Eventually I spoke to him, and he sent me a letter indicating that someone else had patented the same invention. I'm not accusing anyone of taking anything from me. I've tried to put it all behind me. Yet, when I contemplate the matter, I find the sequence of events very ironic."

"Damn," said Jess. "You would think that if a person tries to take credit for someone else's work, the thief would at least have the decency to pretend to be an anonymous benefactor and send a check so the real inventor could get paid, too."

"Yeah, as if that would ever happen," said Danielle.

"Well, my dear friend, there's nothing that I can do about someone stealing your screenplays or your inventions," said Jess. "But I will try to get your letters back while you're in London. I'll go to the nursing home to see Mrs. Sara and find out if she's got them. I will give you the checks, even though you say you don't want them, but I'm keeping the letters."

"Why do you want to read old letters?" Danielle asked.

"Hell, I need something to do while you are away," said Jess.

"I thought you were planning on doing Dr. Jeremy Chambers."

"Chambers—is that his last name?" Jess asked.

"If we are talking about the same person, then that would be his last name."

"I can live with that: Mrs. Jessica Chambers. It has a nice ring to it. The one thing I can say about all that we have gone through is that Maria was right. People who do you wrong always come back with their hands out. Yesterday, Frankie and Cassie came to the shop looking for a job."

"You're kidding," said Danielle.

"I kid you not," said Jess.

"Well, what happened? Did you hire them?"

"Of course, I did. I couldn't disappoint Maria."

"Are you really going to trust those two women in your shop?"

"I didn't say all that, now. I'm not going to let those two buzzards sabotage me. I said that I gave them a job. Safe jobs." Jess laughed.

"My God! Jess, what do you have them doing, sweeping the floor?"

"No, they are my new shampoo girls."

"Shampoo girls? But didn't they graduate from cosmetology school along with you?" Danielle asked. "They have their license to do hair, right?"

"Sure, they do."

"But you have them working as shampoo girls?"

"It's a damn job, isn't it?" snapped Jess.

"Girl, you're cold. Shampoo girls-you might as well have given them a job sweeping the floor. That's what I would have done," said Danielle, laughing.

"Now listen to you. And you call me cold," said Jess.

"I would have bought French maid uniforms for both of them." Danielle laughed.

"Oh, hell no!" said Jess. "I can just see those two fat asses parading around my shop and scaring all my customers away. You know they think their big whale asses are fine?"

Danielle was laughing so hard that she missed her turn into the Broward Mall. She made a U-turn and drove around to Macy's and parked. For some reason, neither of them made any gesture to open the door and get out of the car.

Danielle was thinking about Max and the flight she was taking to London in the morning with Ted. She thought about the Pointer Sisters CD that Jess had given to her as a gift when she started working for the Broward County State Attorney's office. Danielle had to smile when she thought about Jess's handing her the CD and saying, "Now that you're grown, I can give this to you. You got to be a grown woman to handle the Pointer Sisters." She knew that if she told Jess about all the little things that Max did for her and to her, Jess wouldn't make jokes about her going to London and cheating on him with Ted. She was a grown woman, and she was actually living that song on the CD, *A Man with a Slow Hand.*

Danielle was hoping that Max would let her know he was serious about having her in his life. She hoped that tonight Max would make a solid commitment by asking her to marry him. He was her first, and if he asked, she would say yes.

Could he really love me enough to marry me, or could his display of affection be some sort of curiosity about making love to a black woman? Danielle asked herself. Danielle loved and wanted Max. But she needed to know if he truly loved and wanted her. She knew she would never be with Ted or any other man if Max would just give her something to hold onto while she was away. She feared that she could have another Carl Palmer situation on her hands and vowed that she would not be a fool for any man ever again.

Danielle loved Max, and she could not stop herself from thinking about the nights she spent at his house. He would fill the tub with scented bath oils and rose petals whenever she came over, just so she could relax while he was preparing dinner. He had a few tricks up his sleeve about cooking that he had learned from Jackie. Danielle would always fall asleep in the tub, but Max loved taking care of her. After setting the table and cooking dinner, he would go into the master bathroom, grab Danielle's sponge from her hand, and begin to bathe her. He always woke her by softly touching and stroking her thighs, and then she would lean forward as he washed her back.

One time after Max had finished giving her a bath, she looked up at him with tears rolling down her face.

Max, looking concerned, said, "Come on, baby, let's get you dried off." He held her as she stepped out of the tub. Then he took the towel and wrapped it around her. The two of them stood there and looked into each other's eyes. "Now tell me—what's wrong, sweetheart?" Max asked.

"I was just thinking about us and how long all of this would last. I love you, Max, and it scares me. The black man I dated never drew my bath. I dated him for a long time, and all he ever did was hurt me. He and his family have always made me feel as if I wasn't good enough. I tried to understand why I was always invited over there, but I never felt like I was welcome. I would often fight back tears until I was driving home. I thought they treated me so badly because my skin was dark. Perhaps it was because I didn't have the right family background. I dated him for what seems like a lifetime. He even told one girl that he didn't love me, that he never loved me."

Danielle laid her head on Max's shoulder, sobbing. Max's eyes filled with tears. "Your old boyfriend was just being a man by telling the other woman what she wanted to hear. I don't think he ever meant to hurt you. That guy didn't have any intentions of letting you find out about what he had said or of hurting you so badly." He lifted Danielle's head, kissed her, and said, "I love you, baby, and you will never have to worry about being hurt again. I want to take away all your worries and your pain. And speaking of being scared, I'm afraid of your going to London, falling for someone, and forgetting about me."

"Max, are you really worried?" Danielle asked. "Baby, that will never happen."

Max finished drying her off and grabbed Danielle's robe and put it on her. "Come on, let's eat dinner," he said. Max's only desire was to make sure she didn't lift a finger whenever she was with him. And Danielle made sure he was well rewarded when they made love.

Danielle and Jess would sometimes just sit quietly and think after they had a heart-to-heart conversation. They respected each other enough not to pry unless one of them was ready to talk. But being pressed for time, Danielle looked at Jess and asked, "Are you ready to go shopping?"

"You don't have to ask me twice," said Jess.

"Hold up a minute. I want to ask you something."

"Go ahead," Jess said. "Ask me."

"It's really not a question. It's more an observation-based on what you have told me about your ordeal when you were in New York. I believe that you dress like an old woman so men won't find you attractive. Am I right?"

Jess dropped her head and said, "Those girls jumped me in school because of how I looked. My cousin threatened to throw me out on the streets because her boyfriend wanted to have sex with me. I just don't want anybody hating me. I don't want to be accused of something I didn't do. For a long time, I didn't have anyone. I was all alone. I thought if I looked and dressed a certain way, my problems would be few. So far it's been working."

"Well, we're back at Macy's. You are getting a new wardrobe today. So, get out of the car, and let's go shopping. Pick out anything you want. I'm paying for everything. You can't go around looking as if you just don't care. When are you going to Starbuck's again?"

"Today is Saturday, so I won't go there again until Monday morning," said Jess.

"I am picking out an outfit for you to wear the next time you see Jeremy. And he will ask you for a date. You call me in London and tell me about it."

"Do you want to know everything?" Jess asked.

"Hell no " said Danielle. "Max and I make our own porn movies, and we're the star performers. All I need to know is that someone is looking out for you while I'm away. I honestly don't know what I would do if anything should ever happen to you. Besides, I can just imagine what you will be doing with Dr. Jeremy.

"If I'm lucky, probably the same thing as you and Max.," said Jess.

"But, Jess, I need to admit something to you. I'm really scared that I might cheat on Max when I'm in London. I have always been sexually attracted to Ted, but Max was the one who made the first move. I love how Ted looks out for me and how it feels just to be near him. There have been times when we were working late that I wished he would have pushed the files to the side and made love to me on top of the conference table. The few times when I thought he wanted to kiss me, he never made a move. And he knew I was attracted to him."

"Why didn't you make the first move and kiss him?" Jess asked.

"I couldn't do that," said Danielle. "It would have been a Carl Palmer situation all over again. If he wants me, he will have to make the first move."

"Listen to you," Jess said. "You've got *unfinished business* with Ted."

"That's what scares me. I don't want to hurt Max. But sometimes I can't help but think that I have dreamed about Ted making love to me for so long, and whenever it's just the two of us in the office late at night, my stomach always gets all tied up in knots being near him."

"What does he do?" Jess asked.

"He just looks at me and smiles. And then I hold my hands between my legs and rock. He acts as if he thinks that I am cold and begins to rub my arms, and then he puts his coat around me. I push him away and say that I'm not cold."

"That's the problem," said Jess. "The man tries to make a move on you and you stop him. You have been running, but you won't be able to run when he gets you out of the country. You said you want me to tell you if Jeremy asks me for a date; I want to know if you let Ted open your pocketbook, and how many times he opens it. You are going to have a new name when you come back."

"What name will that be?" Danielle asked.

"Santa Claus."

"Max is the only man who has ever touched me. So, one man does not constitute my being a Santa Claus."

"After London, Ted will make two. All you need is a few more back-to-back. You will be well on your way to being a full-fledged Santa Claus."

"Oh! Shut the hell up, Jessica"

"When I pick you up from the airport in two months, I'm going to be singing *Santa Claus is coming to town.*"

"Girl, just be quiet and let's go shopping."

Chapter 9

Danielle and Jess had finished with their shopping, and Danielle had promised Max that she would not be late for their special date. After she dropped Jess off, she headed for his house. Danielle was hoping that Max had not made any dinner reservations. She wanted to spend a quiet evening at home. She really didn't feel well. She was a bit ill at ease about travelling to London with Ted. Danielle had wanted to ask Ted to choose someone else to accompany him on the trip, but she never got around to discussing the matter with him. She was too busy spending time with Max. The last two weeks, Danielle had either stayed at Max's house, or he had stayed the night with her. Now it was too late.

Danielle smiled when she thought about how she'd gone from never having sex to making love every night. Sometimes Max would make love to her two or three times in one night. She didn't have any complaints, and neither did Max. They enjoyed spending every minute they could together. They had been inseparable since the first time they made love. *Can I really be away from Max for two months, and will I miss him? Will I suffer from lack of nookie, as Jess suggested?* Danielle wondered.

She had been introduced to this wonderful new world called making love. If she needed Max to hold her and he wasn't there, would she fall for Ted? This thought terrified Danielle. There were so many questions, and yet she had no answers. Danielle's head was spinning. She pressed the play button on the CD player. Marvin Sapp's song I Believe began to play. Her eyes filled with tears. She knew that having sex before marriage was not behaving like a Christian. Her mother would not be pleased with this sort of behavior.

Danielle had hoped that one day she and Carl Palmer would be together as husband and wife. However, she had known that she had to move on with her life and not allow Carl to waste any more of her time. Carl Palmer would never be faithful enough to make any woman a good husband. He was too much of a man whore. Chasing women was all he lived for.

Danielle was angry every time she thought about how she had allowed Carl to mistreat and hurt her so badly. Danielle thought about the times Carl had invited her to come to his house. She would arrive to find another woman there as well. Often, she was subjected to his talking to other women on the phone, and she would hear Carl tell the woman on the other line, "I love you."

This was very painful and tormenting for Danielle. Yet she continued to remain by his side whenever Carl or a member of his family needed her. She sometimes questioned whether Carl hated her. He certainly never treated her as if she was his girlfriend. Danielle felt that the other women in Carl's life got his love, time, and respect.

On her long drive to meet Max for dinner, Danielle reflected on the day she realized that she was done with Carl. Finally, she had decided to confront him. She was determined to tell him what she was feeling.

"I honestly believe that you take great pleasure in tormenting me," she said.

Carl looked at Danielle and laughed. The fact that he laughed gave Danielle the confirmation she needed. *How did I get here? Why did I let him treat me as if I'm not good enough? Why have I allowed him to treat me as if I am not fit to breathe the same air?* Danielle asked herself. Carl tried changing the subject, but Danielle was persistent in letting him know in no uncertain terms that she loved him.

"I love you, but the day will come when I won't. You're not only going to know when it happens, you're going to feel it as well. Those women are going to cause you to lose something that you can't get back and that something is me. I am not going to let you piss in my face and tell me it's rain."

Carl became very upset and blamed Danielle's tirade on being a typical black woman who can't shut up and just enjoy her man whenever he comes over. "I didn't come here to argue," Carl said.

"I'm not arguing. I am trying to have a discussion."

"I don't feel like talking or discussing anything."

"We need to talk."

"I'm leaving," said Carl.

"Do you want me to say my good-bye now or later?" Danielle asked.

"I'll call you later, or you can call me when you calm down," Carl said as he turned to leave.

Danielle never bothered to ask Carl what he felt like doing, for fear he would tell her that he wanted to have sex. Danielle was not impressed with Carl forever boasting about his ability to give good oral sex. Carl dated a lot of women, and Danielle questioned whether she would ever trust him enough to have sex because he was always taking antibiotics of some sort.

At one point, Danielle needed to know what type of medication he was currently taking just in case the two of them should ever become intimate. She wrote down the name of the pills and went online to confirm her suspicions. Carl had indeed contracted a venereal disease from one of the women. He later confessed that this was not the first time, and that he had taken medication for similar ailments.

Danielle thought about how the women Carl had engaged in oral sex with were the very same women who had given him a venereal disease. There really wasn't a question as to where his mouth had been. The thought of Carl dining between the legs of such filth made Danielle feel nauseated. She couldn't resist letting Carl know that he was such a dumbass. Carl thought that if he had a woman tested, it was okay to have unprotected sex.

"Having a woman tested does not prove a thing," Danielle said one day. "If the test comes back negative, it could mean it hasn't shown up in her system yet."

Danielle warned Carl that he had better be careful going around eating pussy as if he were eating bread. If a woman cheats, chances are you and every other man has eaten another man's semen. Danielle shouted, "You need to find one person to love and be faithful to her. It doesn't have to be me. Do you really think that a woman can't or won't go out and have sex with someone else after you've had her tested? You can do something about ugly, but there isn't a damn thing you can do about stupid. Dumbass.

"I suggest that you start looking at sex the way comedian Renaldo Rey describes it: as a strong affection, a tight connection, and a moment's recollection."

She told Carl that he needed to protect himself if he insisted on having multiple sex partners.

Danielle knew she would never kiss him again. Maybe Carl's telling her that he was good at giving oral sex was his way of trying to seduce her. However, Danielle was not that weak or gullible.

Carl would often tease Danielle about being his wife. More than likely he was also running that same line to the other women in his life. Danielle knew that she was not the only woman for whom Carl had purchased a diamond ring. Danielle was not deluding herself into thinking that a ring from Carl meant anything. It was his way of marking his territory and branding the woman as a damn fool. At times, Danielle felt as if she was lost, confused, and aging in Hell. She did what came naturally and wrote a poem to let Carl know just what he could do with his ring and the lie about seeing her as his wife.

Lost, Confused, And Aging in Hell

What is Hell? Hell has been our marriage
With this you might agree
I was married to you
But you were never married to me
My heart no longer burns with the lingering excitement
Of the love we once shared
And I have doubts that you ever cared
You filled my nights with sadness
Now I long to be in some man's arms
To be kissed, petted, and pampered
To be tenderly made love to all night long
Our marriage is now over, this I feel was meant to be
For I have loved and given for so long
But nothing was returned to me
I have walked in your shadow. I've even walked in your light
Hopefully someday I shall walk into another man's arms at night
I have been to your school of knowledge
And have been taught well
I know that I now live in Heaven
Because I feel no pressure from Hell

Perhaps Danielle's relationship with Carl had forced her to believe that there was no such man as Mr. Right. The way that Carl mistreated Danielle definitely caused her to start thinking about dating white men.

According to Jess, black men would be the first to take offense to her dating a white man. Danielle was hoping that Jessica was wrong about how black men or blacks in general would respond to her dating a white man. Besides, it was the twenty-first century, and people were not so antiquated in their thinking about interracial relationships. Danielle had wanted to be with a black man, but the black man she loved and wanted to spend the rest of her life with had other plans. Thank God not all black men were like Carl Palmer.

Honestly, Danielle didn't care what anyone thought about her dating Max. She had dated a black man who treated her as if she were unimportant and didn't matter. Carl Palmer treated his car better than he treated her. Danielle wished that she had the opportunity to express to black men how some black women would love to be treated. She would tell them to stop criticizing black women, because they had a few complaints of their own about black men's behavior. They really do appreciate a man with a slow hand.

Danielle had it all thought out about how she would make her point by giving a perfect analogy. She would start by saying, "Treat your woman the way you treat your car." Danielle vowed that she would make it very clear that the black women in her monthly book club constantly talked about how they wished their men loved them the way they loved their cars. "The way you wash your car—try giving us a bath and wiping our bodies dry. The way you adorn your car with a set of rims—try buying something for us so we can look nice. The way you wax, polish and rub down your car—try getting the lotion and gently rubbing and massaging our bodies. Rather than just having sex, try making love to us."

Max did all these things for Danielle. He gave her a bath and wiped her dry. He bought her a diamond necklace so that she could look nice. He kissed and gently massaged her body, and then he made love to her. It took a white man to let Danielle know that she was worthy to be loved and that black was beautiful.

Danielle had thought that Carl Palmer would be the first and only man with whom she would ever be intimate. Yet Danielle was glad that she had made the decision to lose her virginity with Max. She had no regrets other than the fact that she was not married to him. This behavior was out of character for her.

Danielle had always believed in God, and she lived the life of a Christian. She was praying that Max would let her know before she left town that he really loved her and wanted her in his life. Danielle needed more than Max screaming out during a moment of passion, "Marry me, Danielle. Marry me." Reflecting on her hurtful past with Carl Palmer made her sad, and she needed Max to hold her and treat her the way a woman should be treated. She needed to hear Max's voice when tears were rolling down her cheek.

She grabbed her cell phone to call Max and let him know that she would be pulling into his driveway soon. Danielle arrived at Max's house, and he walked outside to meet her. Max kissed and held her as if he would never see her again.

"Baby, you've been crying. What's wrong?"

"I'm fine. Just hold me."

"I'll hold you all night."

"I love you, Max."

"I have a special evening planned."

"Is that the reason you insisted that I not be late?"

"I don't want you to ask any questions. Just enjoy everything." '

'Enjoy what?" asked Danielle.

"You'll see. Come inside."

"Max, I hope you didn't make dinner reservations. I just want to be alone with you. I'm tired," said Danielle.

"Of course, you are. I've got your bath and dinner waiting. You can relax in the tub while I set the table."

"That sounds perfect."

"Come on, let's get you inside," said Max.

Max carried Danielle's purse and held her hand as they walked inside. Danielle went into the bathroom and began to undress while Max poured her a glass of wine. Max entered and finished undressing her. He helped her into the tub and handed her the glass of wine. After Max finished setting the table, he went into the bathroom to get Danielle dried off. As he dried Danielle's body, he told her that he had something special to give to her.

"I'll give it to you after dinner," said Max.

Should I give it to her now, or is it too soon? Max wondered. They sat down to a wonderful dinner of grilled pink salmon, asparagus, and baked potatoes. For dessert, Max made a perfect attempt to duplicate the Hard Rock Cafe's hot fudge brownies with walnuts, topped with a scoop of vanilla ice cream. He knew that this was one of Danielle's favorite desserts. After dinner Max cleared the table and suggested that Danielle go into the bedroom to rest. Max noticed Danielle holding her stomach as she was getting up from the table.

"What's wrong, baby? Are you okay?"

"Yes, I think it's just nerves."

"You might be pregnant," Max said.

"You wish. I am not pregnant. We are not going to have any big— feet children running around."

"Big feet?" said Max.

"Yes, you've got huge hands and gigantic feet." Danielle laughed.

Max smiled. "I have always heard black people say that if a man has big hands and feet, he has a large penis. I know you like all of my big attributes."

"Okay, white boy, don't make me wait too long to see your attributes," Danielle said, laughing.

Max rubbed Danielle's stomach, kissed her, and said, "Go lie down and get some rest. You're going to need it."

"Promises, promises," said Danielle.

Max laughed. "You should know not to challenge me."

Danielle stood there looking at Max, as if she was sizing him up.

Max smiled, shook his head, and said, "You are too much."

Danielle smiled back at him and walked into the bedroom.

Max had carried out his plan of having Danielle wake up next to him every morning. She had spent her last two weeks in town in his arms. His next move was to give her his mother's ring and seal the deal. But he hadn't counted on making love four times that night, causing him to miss his opportunity for the perfect moment to give her the ring. What's worse, this would be the last time he saw her before she left. Max didn't want to take Danielle to the airport, because he couldn't bear seeing her get on the plane with Ted. He would rather her friend Jessica handle that task and spare him the torment.

They had just finished making love the fourth time when Danielle's cell phone rang. Jessica was calling to make sure that Danielle was awake. Danielle looked over at Max's alarm clock to see the time. Seeing that it was 4:00 a.m., she suddenly felt overwhelmed. Danielle laid back in Max's arms while she talked to Jess.

"I'm at Max's. I have to go home and shower," said Danielle. "I'm leaving now. I'll be ready to go when you get there. See you soon. Bye."

Danielle rushed to get dressed.

"Take a shower here," suggested Max.

"Everything that I need is at my house."

"What do you need that I don't have here?"

"I need my hygiene items."

"I have everything you need."

"Do you have a disposable douche?"

"No! No! No! I don't have one of those," Max said, laughing.

Danielle picked up her purse and headed for the door. She turned to Max and asked, "What was it that you wanted to give me?"

"You're in a rush, and it's too important to rush."

"Are you sure you want to wait? What is it?"

"It will have to wait until you return."

Max walked Danielle to her car and kissed her goodbye. His heart ached at the thought that tomorrow she would be in London with Ted.

On the drive home, Danielle realized that she was getting upset about all the things Jess had said about black men. She was upset for allowing herself to be pulled into such unfounded rhetoric. How could she listen to someone who had never been with a man?

Danielle knew that Jess meant well and that she was just looking out for her. Nonetheless, Danielle realized that there was something quite wonderful about black men. Especially black men like Jeremy and Benjamin Chambers. They were very protective about the women in their lives. If she were their sister or daughter, they wouldn't care who she was dating as long as she was happy. And she was indeed happy. She'd learned that sex was more than intercourse. Max made poetic love to her, and he catered to her every need. Mostly, Max enjoyed Danielle as a woman. There was nothing he wouldn't do to please her. That was what made Max such a good lover.

Eva, Francois, and Pierre

Chapter 10

When Ted and Danielle arrived in London, they went to the villa where his parents lived: the place where he had grown up. Ted introduced Danielle to his parents, and they instantly fell in love with her. They all enjoyed a nice family dinner in the garden getting to know Danielle and listening to Ted tell stories about how he absolutely loved living in Florida. As the evening wore on, Ted and Danielle went to bed so they could get an early start setting up the London office. From there they settled into a pleasant routine. Each day they drove to the city and returned to the villa for a quiet dinner with his parents.

Danielle looked forward to her weekly call from Jessica to fill her in on how things were going with Jeremy. Jessica seemed to be very happy to be in a relationship. Jess and Jeremy had gone on several dates and it look like it could get serious. *That red dress and new wardrobe was money well spent.* Danielle thought

It was now Friday night, and they had been in London for three weeks, working day and night to get the office ready to start seeing clients. They had just finished working and decided to take a stroll and dine at the sidewalk cafe on the corner.

While they ate dinner, Ted told Danielle that his father was from Ireland. His grandfather had sent his son Gunther, who was Ted's father, to London on a business trip. The man he was to see had a beautiful daughter named Anastasia. When they met, they fell hopelessly in love. After being there a month, Ted's father wrote his grandfather and told him that he would not be returning to Ireland; he was staying in London and getting married.

"How did your grandfather respond to the news?"

"My grandfather wrote back and said he would be arriving in two weeks. When my grandfather arrived, he found that my father had borrowed the money from my mother's father to purchase a building and had already started to make furniture. He had built a large clientele and had over a thousand items in backorders. My grandfather met with my mother's parents. When he saw my mother, he congratulated his son for being smart in love and in business.

My sister Anna and her husband Ramon moved to Ireland to run the business after my grandfather died. It's very quiet at the villa now."

"Yes, it is very quiet and beautiful."

"But it won't be quiet after Anna arrives. She's the wild one. Enjoy the quiet while you can. When she gets here, all of my cousins will be coming by to meet you. I told them about the beautiful black attorney who gave me a run for my money in court."

"Gave you a run for your money? I kicked your butt," Danielle said, laughing.

"Yes, you did," said Ted, nodding in agreement.

They finished dinner. Danielle thought that they were done for the day and would be headed home. That was when Ted mentioned that he needed to get a file from the office.

"Do we have to?" Danielle asked. "I want to take a hot bath and crawl into bed."

"I'll only be a minute. I need to go over some figures."

"All work and no play make Ted a dull boy."

Ted looked at Danielle and smiled. "There's nothing dull about me."

"You could have fooled me," Danielle said, smiling.

They returned to the office. Ted picked up the file and walked into the conference room. He sat down, and Danielle sat next to him. He looked at Danielle and smiled. Then he closed the file and said, "Let me do something that I have always wanted to do."

He stood and began to massage her back. He kissed her on the neck, and she didn't do anything to stop him, nor did she want to. She was dazed by his gentle touch. He began to tell her how much he loved her, and that he had always loved her. He was afraid that she would reject him because he was white. He said that he could handle the rejection better if they were away from the office.

Danielle couldn't believe what she was hearing. He moved downward, kissing her between her breasts. Ted pushed the file, and it landed on the floor. He turned her chair around, picked her up, and put her on the conference table.

"Danielle, I told my entire family about you, and I brought you to London to meet them."

Danielle couldn't think or speak. The way Ted was manipulating her nipples with his tongue—how could any woman think under this kind of pressure?

Ted sat in the chair and began removing her stockings and her undergarments. Oh my God! This dream of his making love to her on top of the conference table was unfolding before her eyes, and she was enjoying every minute of their time together.

Ted pulled her closer to the edge of the table and kissed her between her thighs, causing her body to tremble. He stood, kissing her breasts. Ted held her breasts and squeezed them together as his tongue moved across her nipples.

For a brief moment, she wondered if she should be doing this. But the muscles in her vagina had a mind of their own and begged for his presence to massage and thrill him.

The thoughts of what Jess had said crossed her mind, but she didn't want to think or say anything to anyone. She wanted Ted to know one thing, and that was, "Captain, you've got the wheel." Danielle looked down and saw that Ted's penis was not at all small. She thought about all the stereotypes about white people that were so untrue. White people can't dance. White people can't sing. White men can't jump. And the biggest lie of them all: white men have small penises.

She pulled Ted closer. He climbed on top of the table and. slowly entered declaring his presence with every inch of his manhood. Upon entering, he felt the welcoming joy of perfectly toned muscles tightening around his penis. The muscles inside Danielle's vagina continued to grip his penis, which seemed to drive him wild. He had never felt anything like this before.

"What are you doing to me?" Ted asked. "Why did you make me wait so long? Why have you tormented me for so long? Danielle, tell me, is it good for you, baby?"

"Yes! Oh, yes!" said Danielle.

Just when they were about to climax, Francois, Eva, and Pierre returned to the office. They had planned to work late. When they walked in front of the door to the conference room, they looked in to see Ted and Danielle on top of the table. Ted moved and stroked as if he were gliding across a dance floor. Each time Ted thrust downward, Danielle made the most pleasurable sound they had ever heard a woman make. Ted looked back to see the three of them in the doorway and uttered with difficulty, "Close the door—I can't stop."

Danielle looked up and said, "Please close the door. I don't want him to stop." She looked at Ted and said, "Please! Please don't stop! I have wanted you for so long. I need you now."

How could they stop? They were both in the moment. The one thing that they both longed for was to make love. Pulling out or jumping up was not an option. Yet in the back of Danielle's mind, she wondered. Wow! I never would have thought I would do something like this "

Eva stammered away very upset that Ted was making passionate love to this black attorney he had brought from the States. She had hoped that she and Ted would rekindle their relationship. She had known Ted since they were kids. But from Ted's point of view, he was already in a relationship, all the way into the gripping walls of Danielle's vagina. He and Danielle had longed for this moment, and they were not going let anyone take it away.

Pierre and Francois didn't move from the doorway. They stood there as if they were frozen in time and space. They listened as Danielle sighed and called Ted's name and as Ted said, "Dani, I can't hold back any longer. Your muscles are gripping and squeezing the head of my…you're driving me crazy." Ted and Danielle reached their climax.

Finally, Francois and Pierre walked away smiling. Eva sat in her office sulking. Ted and Danielle lay on top of the table in each other's arms. They were thinking that they had worked day and night to set up the London office, and now that it was complete, they could turn the remaining five weeks into a vacation. Ted thought how he could make their time in London end with many more nights like the one they just had.

Chapter 11

The next day, Ted's mother, Anastasia, walked into Danielle's room to wake her for breakfast. Anastasia sat on the side of the bed, touched Danielle's hand, and said, "Dear, wake up. We can't start breakfast without you."

Danielle opened her eyes, looked up at Ted's mother, and smiled. "Good morning, Mrs. O'Reilly," she said.

"Good morning, dear," Anastasia said. "How about your calling me Mother? Ted told us that you lost your mother, and you are all alone in the world. You don't ever have to worry about being alone; we're your family now. I'll see you at breakfast, so get up and get dressed."

Danielle showered and put on a beautiful, white two-piece suit. She entered the room where everyone was waiting. Ted jumped to his feet and said, "Dani, you're beautiful. Come sit next to me." Danielle took her seat next to Ted.

She looked at him and said, "I didn't mean to interrupt your conversation when I walked into the room. Are you planning some sort of ceremony?"

Anastasia motioned to the housekeeper to bring in the food. Ted was shocked that Danielle had overheard them talking. He wondered how much of the conversation she'd heard. Anastasia rushed to Ted's rescue and said, "No more talking. The food will get cold."

During breakfast, Anastasia told Danielle that the two of them would be going to the city to do some shopping while Ted and his father talked.

"Sure, that would be nice," said Danielle. "I would love to pick up a few things while I'm here. I thought that Ted would take me sightseeing, too. Would you like to go, Ted?"

"No," said Anastasia. "I want to get to know my new daughter. You can take her sightseeing some other time. I would like for Danielle and me to spend some time getting to know each other before your sister Anna gets here from Ireland. The two of you will only be here five more weeks before you return to the States. There is so much to do before you leave."

Danielle felt there was something going on that they were keeping from her. All this talk about a ceremony, taking her shopping and calling Danielle her daughter, and having so much to do before they left made Danielle a little curious. Perhaps the ceremony they were talking about would be a farewell dinner for Ted. This had to be the reason why his sister, her husband, and their two kids were coming to London. Danielle decided not to be paranoid and ruin her trip. She would just go along with the flow of things and see what would happen. *It's probably nothing to worry about*, she thought.

Ted's dad saw how Ted couldn't stop looking at Danielle. He noticed Ted grab Danielle's hand and kiss it. Danielle, however, was embarrassed that he would do this in front of his parents. She eased her hand away from Ted and placed it under the table on her lap. Ted reached under the table and ran his hand up Danielle's skirt. She took a deep breath and sighed. *Oh my God, why did he do that?* Danielle asked herself.

Ted couldn't keep his hands off Danielle. Danielle knew he wanted a repeat of what had happened the night before at the office.

Danielle took her napkin in her left hand and wiped the sweat from her brow. She couldn't believe he had turned her on in the worst way right in front of his parents.

Ted looked at the sweat on Danielle's nose and said, "Here, baby, let me get that for you." He took his napkin and began to wipe away her sweat.

"Is it too warm for you, my dear?" Gunther asked. Anastasia elbowed Gunther and smiled.

Ted took Danielle's hand and got up from the table. "I want her to lie down for a while before she goes shopping."

No one said a word as Ted led Danielle back to her room. He took off her coat and unzipped her skirt. He picked her up and laid her on the bed. Danielle felt like a rag doll whenever Ted touched her. She had longed for him, and now he was doing things to her and touching her in places she had only dreamed he would.

As she lay there, Ted unbuttoned her blouse and placed it neatly on the chair so it wouldn't get wrinkled. He kissed her again and again. He looked down and unfastened her bra, which unsnapped from the front.

"Are you okay?" Ted asked.

Danielle opened her eyes and said,

"Yes."

"You have the most beautifully shaped breast I have ever seen." Ted said.

Ted removed her stockings and kissed her thighs. He pulled her panties down to her knees and laid his head on top of her vagina.

Danielle wondered why he had stopped. She asked, "Are you okay? Is everything all right?"

"Everything is fine, baby. I just can't believe that you are here with me, and I made love to you." Danielle ran her fingers through his hair. Ted looked up at her and said, "I've found the place where I want to be, Dani. I never want to leave, and I don't want you to ever shut me out."

Ted kissed Danielle's thighs and finished taking off her panties. He wanted nothing more than to please her. He kissed and sucked her breasts. Danielle gave a pleasurable sigh. He seemed as if he couldn't stop pulling her breasts gently with his teeth. He went down and started to kiss her vagina, and he inserted his tongue inside while both his hands were still on her breasts. Danielle let out a loud moan.

Ted took his hands and placed them on Danielle's hips so he could feel her body as it moved in a circular motion. Ted continued to dine on Southern cuisine. She was about to have an orgasm when Ted rushed to put his penis inside. He felt the warmth of Danielle's juices all around his penis.

Danielle screamed, "Ted, it's too big You're hurting me. Ted, please slow down."

"I'm sorry, baby. I guess I got carried away. It feels so good when I'm inside of you. I was just too excited." Ted began to move slower. Danielle calmed down and began to enjoy how good it felt. They both came together.

Ted's parents came upstairs to check on them and were listening at the door. When they heard Danielle tell Ted it was too big, they looked at each other and walked away, smiling. They returned to the dining room and waited for Ted and Danielle to come down.

"I have got to find her the perfect dress," said Anastasia.

"She's not going to feel like doing any shopping when they're done," said Gunther.

"We have to go shopping today," said Anastasia. "Anna and everyone will be here tomorrow. We have to get everything ready."

Ted, still lying on top of Danielle, took his penis out and lay down beside her. Danielle got up and straddled him.

He looked at Danielle. "What are you doing?"

Danielle looked at Ted, smiling, and said, "I want to do everything to you that you've done to me. It's my turn to thrill you and give to you all of me."

Danielle held Ted's penis in her hand and kissed it. It became hard as steel. She massaged it gently with her hand. His penis coming back to life so quickly had happened only when he was in college, and never this fast. Even then he would have to take a break before he could get it up again. Not with Danielle.

Being with Danielle was like sitting down for dinner. The food was so good and tasty that he had to ask for seconds. His penis was the plate he held as he asked the cook, "May I have some more, please?" It was so good that he just couldn't get enough; always wanting more and more and more. Ted discovered that he loved dining on Southern cuisine. Especially when he was eating at Danielle's table, where she was the appetizer, the main course, and the dessert.

Danielle did things to Ted that drove him wild. Ted lay there sighing and moaning. She needed him to make love to her now, but she wanted to continue to thrill him with her notable skills of foreplay. She fought back her desire to allow Ted to enter once again into a realm of total ecstasy. She imagined what it would be like straddling Ted and riding off into the sunset. Danielle didn't want to be selfish. She had promised to thrill him, and she would keep her promise. After all, she was a woman who kept her word.

She sucked and kissed his penis. Ted's penis repeatedly touched the back of her throat as if she was going to swallow it. Each time she suctioned him into the back of her throat, Ted screamed. Her tiny mouth tightened around his penis just as her vagina did each time he penetrated her.

Ted's body trembled with excitement. He screamed Danielle's name as he overflowed with joy. He turned to the side, allowing Danielle to lie with her head resting midway on his body sucking him dry. She sucked and swallowed until it was all gone. Not one drop of Ted's milk went to waste. He looked down at Danielle as she lay quietly with his penis still in her mouth and her arm wrapped around his leg. She now knew what it was like to dine at Ted's table. He didn't want to disturb her. She looked so peaceful lying there. But his desire to have her lie in his arms, right next to his heart, overwhelmed him.

"Danielle, come here, baby, and lie next to me," said Ted.

They lay there in each other's arms, just as they had the night before.

Hearing the sounds of pleasure and joy that came from Danielle's room ignited a spark between Ted's parents. Gunther took Anastasia by the hand and led her to their bedroom. Anastasia smiled and thanked God that the passion in her husband had been awakened. Gunther was looking at Anastasia the way he had when they first met.

Anastasia was happy Ted had found a woman like Danielle and that he was in love. He was finally happy and wanted to spend the rest of his life with Danielle. She and Gunther didn't care about the fact that Danielle was black. She was the only woman Ted had ever brought home for them to meet.

Eva didn't count. She was a friend of Anna's who had always hung around. Her parents owned the villa down the road. She came over every day to play with Anna. Anastasia remembered when Eva was just a young girl. Eva was invited to Anna's seventeenth birthday party at the villa.

Late into the evening, Ted walked outside to get some fresh air. Eva went looking for him and found him walking in the rose garden. She put her arms around his waist and turned him to face her. Eva kissed him. Ted refused to kiss her back.

"What's wrong?" Eva asked.

"Do I have to get naked to get your attention?"

"Please don't do that," replied Ted.

"Why are you so distant?"

"I've been accepted to study law in the States. I'm having a pickle of a time trying to convince my parents to let me go."

"London has a top-notch school right here," said Eva.

"My dream is to study in the States," said Ted.

Eva took Ted's hand and pulled him to the back of the flower shed. She kissed him and grabbed his penis. Ted told her to stop. She wanted to put her hand inside his pants, and he wouldn't let her. She unbuttoned her blouse and lifted her bra, exposing her breasts.

"I really don't have time for this. I'm not in the mood for your childish games," said Ted.

"We're not children anymore," replied Eva.

"You're seventeen, the same age as my little sister."

"You're only eighteen, just a few months older than I."

"My birthday is in a few months."

"Who cares?" said Eva.

She placed Ted's hands on her breasts. Ted squeezed Eva's breasts very gently. She began to moan and rub up on him. Ted seemed aroused. He kissed and sucked Eva's breasts, but then he stopped and walked away. She went inside and told Anna how she tried to seduce Ted in the rose garden, and that he behaved as if he wasn't interested.

Eva vowed that one day she would make him her husband. She told Anna that if Ted made love to her, she would get pregnant, and he would have to marry her. The next day at school, Eva told everyone that she and Ted had made out in the rose garden. She explained that the only reason they didn't have sex was because Ted was a gentleman and respected her.

Later, when they had both arrived home from school, Anna sat her brother down to have a heart-to-heart talk. She told Ted to stay away from Eva. Anna explained that Eva already had the two of them married with kids.

"I'm not interested in Eva," said Ted.

"I know you're not," replied Anna. "When word gets around that you didn't bed her, your friends are going to call you a queer. I don't want you to be pressured into bedding her. You don't have to prove your manhood to anyone. You have to leave London before something happens with Eva and she traps you. I don't want her for a sister-in-law. The girl is unstable. You have to go to the States."

"Help me convince Mother," said Ted.

"I will," said Anna.

Ted went to his room to rest before dinner. While he lay in bed, Anna informed their parents about everything. She told them that Eva tried to seduce Ted, and that she feared his friends may call him a queer for not bedding her.

"Eva wants to get pregnant in order to trick Ted into marriage," Anna said. "She knew that if she told everyone that he didn't bed her, they would make fun of him, forcing him to bed her. I know you love him, and that you are going to miss him. I will, too. But please let him go now." Anna started to cry. "Please let him go. If you want him to be happy, if you want him to be safe, let him go, Mother, please."

Ted's parents were furious that Eva had pulled such a dirty trick on Ted. Anastasia told Anna to wake her brother for dinner. Anna rushed upstairs and told Ted that she had talked to their parents about letting him go the States so he could get away from Eva. Ted went into the bathroom to wash up and got dressed for dinner. He entered the dining room, where his parents and sister sat waiting.

Gunther spoke first. "How fast can you pack your bags? You're leaving for the States tonight. Your mother has arranged your flight departure and hotel accommodations. When you land, you must call to inform us that you have checked into your hotel. You have your credit cards and cell phone. I will increase your spending limits and have the bank issue you new cards so you will be able to take care of yourself."

Anastasia and Anna began to cry. Ted walked over to his mother and sister to kiss them good-bye. Ted shook his father's hand and told him thanks.

Gunther put his arms around Ted and held him close. He said, "My son, I love you."

"Father, I'm going to make you proud. I'll keep my head in the books. I won't screw up, I promise." said Ted.

They all stood around hugging each other and crying.

After dinner, Gunther called for the driver to take them to Heathrow airport so they could spend time with Ted before his flight to the States.

Now Ted had returned home under much happier circumstances, and his parents were enjoying having him with them again.

Ted O'Reilly

Chapter 12

Ted and Danielle woke up from their long lovemaking session. They smiled at each other and kissed. She remembered she had to get dressed and go shopping with Ted's mother. But she had not gotten to straddle Ted the first time they made love as she had hoped, so she straddled him, thinking she might have to get him in the mood. To her surprise, Ted was ready again.

"Mother is waiting to take you shopping," said Ted. "Danielle, stop. Let's do this later."

Danielle pleaded and begged until she persuaded Ted to make love to her. She leaned back so Ted could enter, and she began to fulfill the fantasy that Jess had placed so vividly in her mind. The way Danielle moved her hips made Ted scream her name. "Danielle! Oh my God! Danielle."

Anastasia and Gunther left their room and headed back to the dining room. As they passed by, they heard Ted and Danielle going at it again.

"How many times is she going to give it to him?" Anastasia asked.

"He's not complaining," replied Gunther.

They both laughed and continued downstairs and sat at the dining room table. The housekeeper walked out and poured them a hot cup of tea. They all laughed when they heard Danielle scream, "Ted, baby, it feels so good!"

Ted replied, "Danielle, slow down."

"I can't."

"Danielle, you're like a wild woman. Slow down. I'm cutting you off. You're like a beast," said Ted. "You're not getting any more."

Danielle slowed down. "You're not giving it to me again?"

"No, I'm not," said Ted. "You don't need any more."

Danielle contracted her muscles around Ted's penis, and he screamed, "Danielle, it feels so good, baby."

"Are you going to cut me off?"

"No! Baby, never."

"You promise?" Danielle asked, squeezing her vaginal muscles tight onto Ted's penis. "You promise?" she asked again.

"Yes, baby, I promise!" said Ted.

"Come get on top and make me feel as if you'll never stop loving me," said Danielle.

Ted rolled over on top of Danielle. They continued to scream each other's names until they both reached an orgasm.

Danielle jumped to her feet and ran into the shower. She rushed and got dressed, and Ted lay in bed, totally and completely exhausted. He watched her as she got dressed. He was smiling the whole time.

Danielle, fully dressed, asked, "Would you like for me to come back to bed?"

"No! Get out of here," Ted said, laughing.

Danielle, pretending to take her coat off, said, "You look as if you want me to come back to bed."

"Please! Go away and leave me alone." Ted pulled the covers over his head, laughing.

Danielle laughed and tried to pull the sheet off. "Let me get back in bed," she said.

They were laughing and playing like two little kids. "I'm going to leave you alone," said Danielle. "Put your pants on and walk me out." Ted put his pants on and walked Danielle to the dining room, where his parents were sitting.

"Are you feeling better, my dear?" Anastasia asked.

Danielle looked at Ted and smiled. "Yes! I feel much better now."

"Good," said Anastasia. "Let me grab my purse so we can go shopping."

Ted and Danielle walked outside, where the driver was waiting to take them to the city. He opened the door, but Danielle wouldn't get in. She stood there holding onto him as if she would never see him again.

"I'll be here when you get back," he said.

Just as he spoke those words, Eva drove by, looking very upset and angry that Ted was holding another woman in his arms. She must be headed to her parents' home for the weekend, thought Ted. Eva had taken a flat in the city to be closer to work.

Anastasia walked outside and got into the car. Ted watched as they drove off. He went back into the house and sat at the table with his father. Gunther looked at Ted smiling. Ted smiled back.

"I can tell this Danielle makes you very happy," said Gunther.

"Yes, she does," replied Ted.

They sat talking for hours. Ted told his father about his plans to ask Danielle to be his wife. He talked about how Danielle was an only child and how her mother had died while she was at Harvard studying to become a lawyer.

"Is that where the two of you met?" his father asked.

"No, I was long gone when she arrived to begin her studies. I'm telling you about her because I want you to know that Danielle is the most fascinating woman I have ever met. She is flawless. I love everything about her. She has a wonderfully brilliant mind. You must see how she works a courtroom. When she walks into a room, all eyes are on her. She is fair, honest, and so full of love. I don't think she has an enemy in the world. Whenever we spend late nights working in the office, we talk for hours about life, love, and her faith in God.

"I have never shared this with anyone, but there are two reasons why I wanted to open a London office. The first reason was to get Danielle alone so that I could tell her how much I truly love her. I needed to let her know that I have an unbearable longing to wake up each morning with her lying next to me. I was desperate to hold her in my arms and make my intentions known by offering her a proposal of marriage. If I could somehow get her to marry me, it would eliminate the competition when we return to the States.

"Secondly, if she should turn down my marriage proposal, I would have no choice but to stay here and run the London office. I would not return to the States. I honestly don't know if I could live without her. Surely, I couldn't return to the States and work in the same office with her. Although I don't have anything concrete to go on, I believe that Max may have fallen in love with her as well."

Ted told his father that the only person close to Danielle was her best friend, Jessica. They had been inseparable since childhood, until Jessica's grandmother passed, and Jessica was forced to move to New York with an abusive relative.

"Danielle was very worried about leaving her friend Jessica, whom she loves and takes care of like a little sister. I can always tell when Danielle has something weighing heavily on her mind. I knew that something was troubling her, and she wouldn't tell me so that I could take care of her and handle the problem. Danielle spoke to Jessica on Monday for their weekly talk. However, on the drive home last night she broke her silence and shared with me that she had been calling Jessica for two days, and that Jessica had not answered her phone."

"Has she spoken to anyone who could tell her about the welfare of her friend? Why is there this great need for concern?" asked Gunther.

"Apparently, Danielle gave Jessica thirty thousand dollars to buy out an unsavory business partner. This woman tried to skip town with her boyfriend without signing the papers that the transaction ever took place. Now Danielle is concerned that this woman will come to realize that the papers she thought she was signing for supplies was actually the sales contract. When they figure out that their scheme was fouled, they may return and attempt to harm Jessica."

"My word, you don't say," said Gunther.

"I placed a call to our office manager, Jackie, and asked her to have a retired police officer who is a friend of ours work security at Jessica's shop."

"What about when she goes home for the evening?" asked Gunther.

"I took care of that as well."

"What did you do to remedy the situation?"

"I hired a personal bodyguard to be with her whenever she is away from the shop. At least this will keep Jessica safe until we get back to file the paperwork to get restraining orders for her protection."

"I am very happy to hear you are concerned about Danielle's friends."

"It gives Danielle peace of mind to know Jessica is safe," said Ted.

"A woman will love a man when he is compassionate and cares about the things that are important to her."

"I love Danielle, Father, and I would do anything in the world for her."

"Have you discussed marriage?"

"We have talked about what we would like to have in a marriage, but never about the two of us being married."

"You can't wait on things to just happen," said Gunther.

"We never kissed before coming here. I couldn't ask her to marry me without knowing if she really loved me."

"What about now?" asked Gunther.

"Now I feel as if I have a chance."

"I didn't wait around when I met your mother."

"I know you didn't. I know how you jumped into action when you first laid eyes on her," said Ted.

"Your mother and I are not getting any younger. I would enjoy having at least five more grandchildren," said Gunther.

"Five! Father, are you serious?"

"Very serious, I might say."

"Are you trying to turn Danielle and me into a couple of rabbits?"

"I'm doing quite the contrary." Gunther laughed.

"Danielle and I will never get out of bed," said Ted.

"That seems to fit your schedule very nicely."

"Father, we both have careers."

"I'll reduce your number to two boys and two girls."

"Thanks, that really is kind of you. Anna can give you one more by having a little girl to keep those men in the house in line."

"Yes, little girls are very bossy. It was never your mother telling us what to do. Princess Anna gave the orders in this house," said Gunther.

"If Danielle accepts my proposal, we'll get started making babies right away," said Ted.

"She is going to need her strength in order to carry a baby, so I suggest you let her eat breakfast before you take her back to bed." Gunther laughed.

Ted let out a jolly laugh. "I promise I'll take good care of her, Father."

A car pulled into the driveway. Ted got up to see who was outside. It was Anna and her family. They were not expected until tomorrow. Ted ran out to meet them. He was so happy to see his little sister.

"I know that we're a day early. But I couldn't wait to see the woman who has captivated my big brother's heart," said Anna.

"She's not here at the moment."

"Where is this beautiful lady you have been telling me about?"

"Mother took her shopping," said Ted. "Mother wanted to pick out a special dress for the ceremony."

"When I talked to you last week, you said you were going to ask her. Would you like it if I talk to her to see how she feels about all of this?"

"Yes, I would like that very much."

Ted and Anna walked to the rose garden to talk and make plans.

"Mother tells me your Danielle is a beautiful young girl."

"She is twenty-six, and she makes me very happy. She embodies everything that I respect and desire in a woman," said Ted.

"That makes me very happy to hear. What is this I hear about Eva working in your office?"

"I hired an agency to find three attorneys. I asked for two males and one female. If I had done the hiring, I would never have chosen Eva. She makes Danielle feel nervous. I don't want anyone around who makes her uneasy."

Ted and Anna continued to sit in the garden and talk. As Anna spoke, Ted looked at her and smiled. This is what they used to do when they were younger. The two of them would come home from school, and Anna would tell Ted stories about everything that had happened that day. Nothing had changed. Although Anna lived in Ireland, she still kept in touch with all her friends from school. Ted felt as if he had never left. He was happy to be home.

Chapter 13

Anastasia and Danielle returned from shopping, and Danielle went to her room to put her bags down. She looked out the window and saw Ted sitting in the rose garden talking to a very pretty woman. Ted and the woman seemed to be having a great time laughing and talking. Danielle was laughing just watching Ted having so much fun. Ted and Anna looked up and saw Danielle standing at the window. He threw her a kiss and gestured for her to join them.

Danielle entered the garden where Ted and the woman were sitting. "Hello " Danielle said, smiling. "I watched and laughed at the two of you for a while. I enjoyed seeing you have so much fun."

"Do you know who I am?" Anna asked.

"No, I have no idea," replied Danielle.

"You weren't jealous to see him holding hands and talking with another woman?" Anna asked.

"He was having fun and enjoying himself. It made me happy to see him laugh."

"I see why you all love her," said Anna.

"Now that we have all the questions out of the way, Danielle, this is my little sister Anna."

"I am so glad to finally meet you. You are very beautiful," said Danielle.

"I really like this girl. What did you and mother buy from the store?" Anna asked.

"We picked out a beautiful, white chiffon dress," said Danielle. "She said it was for a very special event taking place here in the garden tomorrow."

Ted put his arms around Danielle and kissed her. Anna smiled as she watched the two of them.

"Let's go inside," said Anna. "I want you to meet my husband and my kids."

Later that evening, Anna advised Ted to go through with the ceremony. She didn't see any need for her to talk to Danielle.

Chapter 14

It was Sunday morning, and everyone was busy getting ready for the special ceremony. Danielle didn't know what type of ceremony was going to take place, but it was important enough to bring Anna and her family all the way from Ireland. She also wasn't sure why Ted had stayed away from her all night. Ted, Gunther, and Ramon had gone into the study right after dinner, but she got tired and went to bed. Danielle lay awake waiting for Ted to come in and kiss her goodnight. She didn't want to pry. She dared not ask any questions.

It was now 11:45 a.m., and she still hadn't seen Ted. She knew that they would tell her if he was hurt. Nonetheless, she felt very sad. She missed Ted, and no one was telling her anything about his whereabouts. The ceremony would be starting at noon.

Anastasia walked in to tell Danielle to hurry and put on the white chiffon dress that they had picked out yesterday, and to bring the bouquet of flowers on the table.

Danielle went into the room to put on the white chiffon dress. She walked over to the closet to take out the dress, but she really didn't feel like wearing it. She wanted to wear something that would complement her figure. She took out the black, ankle-length sweater dress instead.

Undecided, she looked out the window to see what everyone else was wearing. She saw Ted walking into the garden with his father and Ramon. Each one wore a white tux. Danielle felt a little nervous that she didn't know anything about this secret ceremony. Why was Ted wearing a white tux?

Perhaps Ted's parents were renewing their marriage vows. Maybe Ted was getting married to some beautiful English socialite he was in love with. No, that couldn't be it. Ted loves me. He wouldn't hurt me like that, she thought. That's something Carl Palmer would do. Danielle, fearing the unknown, decided to call Jess. Talking to Jess would calm her nerves. Danielle had been so busy that the two of them had not talked since Monday. She got her cell phone from her purse and called Jess. "Hello!" said Jess.

"Hi, Jess, where have you been? I have been calling you since Thursday. I need to talk. I'm so nervous and scared."

"What's wrong, Dani?" Jess asked. "Do you need me to come get you?"

"No, I'm okay, I guess. It's just that Ted's family has planned some sort of secret ceremony in the rose garden. His mother bought me this beautiful, white chiffon dress that she insists that I wear today," said Danielle.

Jess started laughing and said, "Dani, put the dress on and go." "No, I wanted to wear my black sweater dress," replied Danielle.

Jess, still laughing, said, "Dani, put the dress on and don't keep them waiting. The ceremony is for you."

"How do you know it's for me?" Danielle asked.

"Dani, I'm at work. I have to wash the perm out of this woman's hair. I need for you to listen to me. Put on the dress and go to the ceremony. Have some fun and call me later. I want to hear all the details."

Danielle could still hear Jess laughing as she hung up the phone. Jess's laughter put Danielle at ease. Danielle suddenly noticed that she had a missed call. It was from Carl Palmer. He had left Danielle a message apologizing for all the pain and hurt that he had caused her.

Danielle finally got the chance to hear Carl say that he regretted losing her. Carl needed Danielle to know that he still loved her.

"I am not happy," said Carl. "I have not had a moment of peace since losing you. I think about you night and day. Every waking moment and even in my dreams, I think about you. I love you, Danielle. Please call me when you get this message. Good-bye."

Danielle finished listening to Carl's message and threw the phone on the bed. She put on the white chiffon dress and grabbed the bouquet of flowers on her way to the garden.

Danielle arrived at the entrance to the garden. Ted's father greeted her and walked her inside. There were people seated in chairs on both sides of the garden's courtyard. She and Gunther walked down the aisle on a long, white carpet that led to where Ted stood. She wanted to run into Ted's arms, but she wasn't sure what she should do. Danielle couldn't take her eyes off Ted. He was one fine white man.

As she got closer, Ted kneeled down on one knee and said, "Danielle, would you please make me the happiest man alive and marry me? Right here. Right now."

Danielle looked around at all the guests, and for the first time she remembered what Max had said: "I'm afraid of your going to London, falling for someone, and forgetting about me." She thought about her talk with the waiter who told her that Ted would make his intentions known.

Ted dropped his head as though he was embarrassed that she might say no in front of all of his family and friends. Danielle could not cause him any pain. She knew she loved Max, and she also loved Ted. Danielle was faced with a dilemma that would be life-changing. Where was her relationship with Max headed?

Ted hadn't even given her a chance to think about marrying him. For him to go this far and set up all of this showed his commitment to her.

So she said, "Yes I'll marry you."

Ted stood up and hugged Danielle as if he was holding on for dear life. He kissed her. Tears rolling down his face, he looked into Danielle's eyes and said, "With every beat of my heart and every breath I take, I will always love you."

Danielle, looking at Ted as her eyes filled with tears, knew she had made the right decision to marry him. She knew she would be happy with Ted. She had a family now. They welcomed her into their hearts and their home.

After the ceremony, Ramon, who stood in as Ted's best man, shouted how Ted had to get busy providing two nieces because he had only boys. Anastasia corrected the count and said she needed at least five more grandchildren. Everyone was laughing and dancing. They were all having a great time.

Gunther took Ted to the side to tell him the same thing his father had once told him. "I'm proud of you, my son. You were wise in business and in love."

Anastasia went to the house to get more ice for the drinks and saw Eva's car parked on the side of the roadway. Eva looked up, saw Anastasia, and quickly drove off. Anastasia didn't think it was important enough to mention to the others.

Ted decided to have one last dance with Danielle before going inside to rest and pack for their honeymoon. He couldn't wait until the music stopped. He picked Danielle up into his arms to carry her into the house. When they reached the driveway, they saw Eva passing the house, driving very slowly. She looked infuriated to see Ted being intimate with someone other than her.

Ted carried Danielle to the bedroom with her head perched on his shoulder. He told her that he had already planned their itinerary. They would leave in the morning for a two-week honeymoon in Paris. They would then travel to Ireland to spend a week with Anna and return to

London to spend the last two weeks with his parents before heading home to the States.

Danielle was excited and loved how Ted just took charge of everything. He took the suitcases from the closet to get her packed first.

"Is that for me?" Danielle asked.

"Of course. These are your bags," replied Ted.

"I'm not talking about the suitcases," she said, pointing to the front of Ted's trousers. She laughed and said, "I'm nicknaming you Ready Teddy."

"This only happens when I'm around you," said Ted.

"What are we going to do about it?" Danielle asked.

"Nothing," replied Ted. "We've got the rest of our lives to make love."

After getting Danielle's things together, they finished up in Ted's room. They then joined the rest of the family in the dining room. Everyone stood and applauded as Ted and Danielle walked in holding hands. As the evening wore on, the family began to retire for the evening.

Ted decided to go back to the office that night because he wanted to get an early start before the Monday morning rush hour traffic. Ramon offered to take care of whatever he needed to get done, but Ted insisted that he needed to handle the matter. He had a letter addressed to Eva, letting her know that her services would no longer be needed.

Danielle pleaded with Ted not to go to the office. "What is it that you feel can't wait until we've returned?"

"I won't be long," replied Ted.

"I'm going with you," said Danielle.

They walked outside to get in the car and drove off. Little did they know that Eva was parked down the road with her lights off, hoping that Ted and Danielle would leave to celebrate their wedding nuptials. They arrived at the office, and another car stopped about ten feet away on the passenger side. Before Ted could walk around to open Danielle's door, a shot was fired. He rushed to open the door and saw that Danielle was bleeding from a wound to the head. He held her, crying. He grabbed his cell phone, dialed 999, and told the operator that his wife has been shot.

Ted looked around to see where the shot came from. Eva was walking toward him with a gun in her hand, ordering him to hang up the phone.

"Hang up," demanded Eva.

"No! What have you done?" yelled Ted. "Are you crazy?" "You were supposed to marry me. You love me."

"No, I love Danielle."

"Leave her. You're coming with me."

"You're crazy! I'm not going anywhere with you. I'm not leaving my wife," snapped Ted.

"You don't want to leave your precious wife? Stay here with her then," Eva said.

She raised the gun and shot Ted three times. After the first shot to the chest, Ted grabbed and held onto Danielle's hand. Eva fired a second shot, and he slid to the ground. Ted looked at Eva in disbelief as she shot him in the head. Eva was determined that if she couldn't have him, no one would.

The police and ambulance arrived and rushed to help Ted and Danielle. They handcuffed Eva and took her to jail. One of the officers who had arrived on the scene was Ted's cousin, Peter. He had been at the wedding ceremony earlier that day.

Peter was overtaken with grief as he placed the call to the villa.

Ramon answered the phone.

"Hello," said Ramon.

"There's been an accident," sobbed Peter.

"Who is this? What do you mean? What accident?"

"It's me, Peter. Ted and Danielle have both been shot. We have arrested Eva," said Peter.

Ramon repeated what Peter had said to him in shock. Anna screamed with pain, while Gunther began pounding the dining room table.

"Lord, help us. My son, my son, my wonderful son."

Anastasia ran out of the bedroom to see what all the commotion was about. Ramon told her about the shooting and that the police had Eva in custody. She collapsed to the floor, screaming.

"She was here today. She was parked outside during the ceremony," said Anastasia.

"Who?" Anna asked,

"Eva was here," replied Anastasia.

"Mother, please don't tell me that you saw Eva stalking Ted and you said nothing?" sobbed Anna.

"Thanks for calling, Peter. We're on our way," said Ramon. They arrived at the hospital to find that Ted was dead, and Danielle was in a coma fighting to survive. They had both suffered bullet wounds to the head. The prognosis for Danielle didn't look promising. The attending physician explained that they had put a call in to the States to have a trauma specialist fly in to operate and remove the bullet.

"Does the young lady have any family?" the doctor asked.

"We're all the family she has," said Anastasia.

Anna remembered Max, Ted's best friend from law school who visited with Ted one summer. It was late, but she couldn't wait until morning. She called Max to give him the sad news. Hearing that Ted and Danielle had married and been shot on their wedding day proved to be too much for Max. He hung up the phone and sobbed in agony. Max knew that Danielle being alone in London with Ted could somehow bring him bad news, but not like this. This was more devastating than he could ever imagine. He'd much rather that they were happily married than hurt in anyway.

Max, still crying, called Jessica to let her know that Danielle had been hurt and that he was leaving on the next flight to London. "I thought you might want to be there," said Max.

"You're damn right I want to be there," replied Jess.

"I'll call to make reservations and call you with the flight plans," said Max.

Dr. Jeremy Chambers, MD – Trauma Surgeon

Dr. Benjamin Chambers, MD-OBGYN

Chapter 15

As soon as Max boarded the plane and took his seat, he looked over and saw Jeremy sitting to his left.

"Jeremy, what are you doing on this flight?" Max asked.

"I've been called to London on an emergency," said Jeremy. "What sort of emergency?"

"An apparent shooting victim," said Jeremy. "Can you give me any details?" Max asked.

"I was told that a couple was shot on their wedding day. The husband died, and the wife is fighting for her life," said Jeremy. "What is it with all the questions? Do you know these people?"

"I believe that the woman you're going to operate on is Danielle," said Max.

"Danielle, your Danielle? Why is she married to this other man?" Jeremy asked.

"I don't know how it happened. What I do know is that I still love her." Tears rolling down his face, he begged Jeremy to save Danielle's life. "Please promise me you'll save her life and bring her back to me. Please."

"As your brother, I promise that I will do everything in my power to save her life."

Jessica walked up just in time to hear Jeremy call Max his brother.

"Jeremy, Max, do you two know each other?" Jessica asked.

"Yes, we do," said Max. "Jeremy, this is Jessica, Danielle's best friend.

"Wait a minute, you're telling me that your girlfriend Danielle and your friend Dani is one and the same? Wow, this really is a small world," said Jeremy.

"Why don't I sit down so the two of you can tell me all about this small world of ours."

Chapter 16

Jeremy, Max, and Jessica arrived at the hospital.

"My name is Dr. Jeremy Chambers. I'm here at the request of your chief of surgery, a Dr. Myles Ferguson."

"Yes, Dr. Chambers, please come with me. Dr. Ferguson has been awaiting your arrival."

Jeremy gave Jessica a kiss and hugged Max. He asked that they wait in the waiting room until he examined Danielle and reported back.

Max and Jessica walked into the waiting room and saw Ted's family waiting for news on Danielle's condition. He introduced Jessica as Danielle's sister. Max knew that with Ted gone, Ted's family was Danielle's only living relatives. There would be no way that they would allow Danielle to return to the States with Max. Jessica would be his ace in the hole to get Danielle back into his life. Max had Jessica and one million dollars in a briefcase chained to his wrist. He had come prepared to wheel and deal, another vice he had learned from his father.

Jessica was the first card he laid on the table. Now Max wondered if he would need to use the money to get what he wanted. He had brought enough money just in case he had to bribe the doctor whom Anna had told him was arriving from the States. That was no longer the case, since his brother Jeremy was the doctor.

Max looked up to see Jeremy heading their way and rushed out to him. "I introduced Jessica as Danielle's sister. I'm not asking you to tell a lie; just don't say anything."

Jeremy walked in and introduced himself. He knew that he would do anything to help Max. "Hi, my name is Dr. Jeremy Chambers. I'm the trauma specialist who was flown here to perform the operation. From what I can tell, the bullet entered from the right side of her head and is lodged near the brain. There has been some brain tissue damage. The prognosis on saving her life looks good. On the other hand, because of the bleeding, I am also sure that there will be some-or even total- memory loss. What I'm trying to tell you is that when she wakes up she may not remember any of you. My priority is to save her life.

Jessica broke down, crying uncontrollably. "She has to remember me. She's all the family I have. She can't forget me," cried Jessica.

"Timing is everything. I have to go and operate to remove the bullet. I'll return to give you an update when I'm done," said Jeremy.

As he was leaving the waiting room, the nurse stopped him and handed him the chart on the blood work he had ordered on Danielle. Jeremy took the chart from the nurse and began to look it over. Her blood was type 0, and her pregnancy test was positive. Jeremy knew he needed to protect Max. He had to make sure that for now, no one else would be made privy to the information in Danielle's chart.

"Did you read this chart? Did you show it to anyone?" Jeremy asked.

"No, it was brought up from the lab and placed in my hands.

I immediately brought it to you," said the nurse. '

'Why? What's wrong?"

"Nothing," said Jeremy. "I don't want anyone giving the family any news unless it comes from me."

"That's not the way we do things around here," the nurse said.

"The doctors are the only ones allowed to speak to the family regarding a patient."

"That's good," said Jeremy, smiling.

The nurse smiled back. After giving Jeremy the chart, the nurse headed back to the nurse's station. Jeremy was so good looking that she couldn't stop herself from looking back. She turned to get one last look at Jeremy and walked into the corner of the wall that lead around to the nurse's station.

Jeremy took the test results from the chart and placed them in his pocket. Then he walked away and went in to scrub for the operation.

After the operation, he returned to the waiting room to let everyone know that it was a success.

"The next seventy-two hours will tell us what we are dealing with as for as her pulling through," said Jeremy.

"There is nothing any of you can do here. I want all of you to go home and get some rest. Jessica, I have arranged for a room here in the hospital, so you can stay with Danielle. Max, I had the nurse set us up in the hotel across the street."

They all hugged and said their goodbyes for the evening. Once they were gone, Jeremy pulled out the report that he had taken from Danielle's chart. "There is something I must tell the two of you. Danielle is pregnant," said Jeremy.

"How far along is she?" Max asked.

"There is no way to tell without a complete exam. The only proof that I have to substantiate the pregnancy is her blood work."

"Max is the father," said Jess. "Dani was never with Ted before this week. I called her every Monday at 10:00 am, which is 3:00 pm. London time. I spoke to her again on yesterday when she was having a problem trying to decide what to wear. During our weekly call on Monday all she talked about was how much she missed Max and I wanted to tell her about my date with you, Jeremy. She told me she loved and missed you, Max. She hasn't been with Ted before this week. It's your baby. Don't you know that?"

"I know it's mine," replied Max. "Jessica is right. She's only been here three weeks. I talked to her every day the first two weeks. Whatever happened between her and Ted had to have taken place this week. But I can never let Ted's family know she was with me before she was with Ted. I won't do anything to tarnish her reputation. When Ted's family finds out that she is pregnant, they are going to naturally assume that Ted is the father."

"You don't have to worry about that. I have the only copy of the test results," said Jeremy.

"What about the hospital computer files?" Max asked.

"That's where you come in. I'll get you to a computer so you can hack away and change the test results," said Jeremy. "Jessica, I need you to move into the room with Danielle. Don't let anyone come in to draw blood or take urine samples. I'll destroy the samples in the lab that belong to her. We each have a job to do. Are we ready?"

"We're ready," said Max.

"I'm ready," said Jessica.

"Jeremy, I really need to see Danielle," said Max.

"Max, I just need the two of you to trust me. We have less than two hours to get this done. The hospital will be changing shifts soon. Our faces are familiar to everyone on this shift because we came in together. We don't want to do anything that would arouse suspicion. I have planned every detail. I can move around the hospital with a comfortable amount of ease with the staff that's now on duty. I won't have that freedom when the shift changes.

"By the way, your introducing Jessica as Danielle's sister was pure genius. We need Danielle's blood relative to decide whom she wants on the case as her physician and whether she leaves here and returns to the States. I just performed some of my best work in that operating room.

When she is strong enough to travel, we are taking your girl home alive and well."

Max's worst fears had come to pass. Danielle had come to London and fallen for another man. Max knew that it was his child she carried. He didn't know the events that had caused her to succumb to Ted's charm, but he was willing to do whatever it would take to make her fall in love with him all over again. Danielle's losing her memory could prove to be a good thing. At least he wouldn't have to compete with Ted's ghost. Max felt that God had smiled on him and given him a second chance to spend the rest of his life with the woman he loved, and together they would raise their child. His only concern now was whether Ted's family would interfere and try to stop him from taking Danielle back to the States.

www.ingramcontent.com/pod-product-compliance
Lightning Source LLC
LaVergne TN
LVHW040146080526
838202LV00042B/3042